SPANDAUERSTR.

Tower

KURFÜRSTENSTR.

Havel River

BASSIN PLATZ

AM BASSIN PLATZ

TÜRKSTR.

NEUE KÖNIGSTR.

AM WILHELM PLATZ

WILHELM PLATZ

FRANZÖSISCHESTR.

Tower

TÜRKSTR.

BABELSBERG

NAUENERSTR.

THE   KANAL

BERLINERSTR.

BURGSTR.

WERTFEGER

KAISERSTR.

STR.

Old Market

N

W   E

S

TOWN PALACE

HUMBOLDTSTR.

Kaiser-Wilhelm Bridge

tgarten

BAHNHOFSTR.

HAUPTBAHNHOF

LEIPZIGERSTR.

POTSDAM, GERMANY
1944

AREA OF
OLD CITY

CHAZAUD

THE
BITTEREST
AGE ❖ ❖ ❖

THE BITTEREST AGE ❖ ❖ ❖ ❖

RAYMOND KENNEDY

TICKNOR & FIELDS ❖ *New York* ❖ 1994

TO GLORIA AND BRANWYNNE

For information about permission to reproduce selections
from this book, write to Permissions, Ticknor & Fields,
215 Park Avenue South, New York, New York 10003.

Library of Congress Cataloging-in-Publication Data

Kennedy, Raymond A.
    The bitterest age / Raymond Kennedy.
        p.   cm.
    ISBN 0-395-68629-6
    1. World War, 1939–1945 — Germany — Potsdam — Fiction.
    2. Soldiers — Germany — Family relationships — Fiction.
    3. Potsdam (Germany) — History — Fiction.
    4. Girls — Germany — Potsdam — Fiction.
        I. Title.
    PS3561.E427B57   1994
    813'.54—dc20   93-30337
                            CIP

Printed in the United States of America

BP 10 9 8 7 6 5 4 3 2 1

Book design by Anne Chalmers
Endpaper map by Jacques Chazaud

THE
BITTEREST
AGE ❖ ❖ ❖

Ursula was in labor; she was sweating freely, and with every contraction gave a soft moan. Nurse Boldt came and went at the door of the room every minute or so. Her presence was reassuring. Ursula's eyes followed her.

"What would I do without you?" she managed to say.

"You would do very nicely," said Nurse Boldt.

Ursula was moving her head from side to side. "I don't think so."

From the delivery room where she lay, she could see all the way to the treetops in front of the Charlottenburg Gate. The sound of the late afternoon Berlin traffic arose to the windows.

When the time came, Nurse Boldt was followed into the room by the doctor. He was a grave, cold-faced man in spectacles who seemed not to smile. Ursula liked his professional look. She trusted him. The rhythmical pain was intensifying. By an irony, Ursula reached and set her fist against her temples in the exact way that her child-to-be would do in future times when in worry or stress.

In the final throes of labor, the nurse was gripping her hand. Ursula was gaping at the ceiling. She wished Walter were here. He was in the corridor. Nurse Boldt told her to push. She said it many times. "You're going to meet each other now. The baby is coming."

She could feel the doctor working. She could feel it all

happening. The first wave of relief was indescribable. It went down the length of her body; it was followed by another, and a third. The baby was in passage. She could feel it moving out alive from her. Wave followed wave of relief.

Ursula lay on her back exhausted; she felt she had given birth to a sky, or an ocean, something of no ordinary dimensions. Through sweated eyes, she saw the baby aloft before her. The doctor was holding the infant by the ankles. There was a tinny yowl, the baby wriggled violently, and then cried out. Ursula couldn't take her eyes away from it.

It was a girl.

1

INGEBORG was a bookworm. Even when they lived on Fasanenstrasse in Berlin, more than two years ago, when she was only eight, she was capable of reading entire books. Whenever her mother anticipated a tiring wait and possible boredom, she would tell Ingeborg to bring her book. Ingeborg's brother, Andreas, who was six, was another matter altogether; being naturally more restless and demanding of attention, he often became the target or subject of Ingeborg's frostiest side. He paid attention, too; he listened to her. In his heart, Andreas was more apprehensive of his ten-year-old sister than he was of his mother, because in his mother's eyes there was always a mitigatory light that softened any spoken displeasure. Ingeborg was not tolerant of noise, high jinks, or any sort of babyish antics. She would just give him a look!

They were living at this time in Potsdam, situated less than twenty miles from Berlin, in a one-room apartment that overlooked a neighbor's vegetable garden. Often while sitting by the window, reading, Ingeborg saw the man from across the way come outdoors to work in his garden. His name, she knew, was Herr Welt. He always took off his glasses when he came outside, and later put them on again when he had finished with his work, tending his beet rows, potatoes, beans, and cabbages. It was a small garden, and Ingeborg was amazed at how the stoutish, balding man could find anything useful to do there every day. He fussed over each plant as though it were a living treasure. Ingeborg did not look with approval upon someone wasting time. Anyhow, the book in her hands was much more compelling. At ten years of age, she was reading adult novels now. Best of all, she liked stories with heroines, women who were beautiful and courageous, and, in the end, managed to save the day. She lost herself in her romances. This was particularly the case these days, as from week to week she saw the look of worry deepening in her mother's face.

There was much talk these days about the severity of the coming winter. Even Frau Redeker, who was Ingeborg's teacher at school (and who was always able to produce another book or two for Ingeborg to borrow), even she had said it, that this winter would be "a trial and a test for all of us." Such talk filled Ingeborg with deep misgivings. She tried not to think about it. She remembered how last year, the winter of 1943–44, her mother had had to skimp with the coal ration, and how they had taken to going to bed very early in the evening to conserve fuel. Mornings, her mother, Ursula, got up first and put papers and bits of wood in the porcelain stove, and then added chunks of coal, one by one, putting them in place with great exactitude, as if she were decorating a cake. The one room in which they lived had two beds, situated along adjoining walls. Andreas shared the slightly larger bed with their mother, while Ingeborg slept on the narrow cot by the side window. When they first came here, Ursula slept on the narrower bed, with the two children in the other one, but Ingeborg would not abide Andreas's fidgeting. He squirmed and fidgeted even while he was alseep, she said.

The room in which the three of them lived was the upstairs corner room of a house that belonged to a certain Dr. Falke, a middle-aged bachelor. The doctor, like Ingeborg's own father, was away in the east, in the war. Annaliese, Dr. Falke's unmarried sister, occupied the remainder of the house. Whenever Ingeborg encountered the woman, when going in or out at the downstairs front door, or when passing in the street, she was always noticeably polite, because she deduced, from what her mother had said, that there would be no place else for them to live if the woman downstairs asked them to leave. Housing was getting scarcer and scarcer. Two summers ago, following three nights of air raids over Berlin, Ursula had tried desperately to find a home for herself and the two children somewhere outside the city; it was only through the help of an old friend of Ingeborg's father that she had been able to find this house. Since then, Ingeborg had often recalled, with a sinking sensation, the sharp disappointment she felt when they came up the stairs and into this room on that summer day.

In Berlin, they had had three spacious rooms, with high ceilings, picturesque windows that overlooked the street, and a sunlit kitchen with closets and cupboards. There were radiator pipes that brought up the heat, a brass mail slot in the door, and shiny brass fixtures and doorknobs everywhere. They had very pleasant neighbors who looked upon them with affection and respect. Here, their circumstances were much reduced. Ingeborg didn't have her original bed, for one thing; her mother had sold it in Berlin to another tenant, along with two easy chairs, their sofa, a pretty Persian carpet, the dining table and the matching chairs with the ribbon-striped seats, and, most precious of all to Ingeborg's eye, the bookcase with the glass doors which stood between the windows above the street. But the furnishings in this room were few. There were no paintings on the walls, no carpets, no hidden cabinets to keep china. There were four walls and two windows; the big porcelain stove looked a hundred years old. There was a sink, a makeshift gas stove, two small beds with rolled-back mattresses on them, a table and chairs.

Ursula had done her best to make the place cozy and livable. There was a pretty lamp on the table and embroidered pillows on the two beds. On one wall there was a photo of Ingeborg's father, Walter Maas — he was wearing his army uniform — and over the table in the corner another dozen or more framed photographs, including a wedding picture of Ursula and Walter, taken on a walkway in the Tiergarten in Berlin, in 1932. There was a picture of Ingeborg in white baby clothes, which looked like little bloomers on her, and which she could never imagine having worn. Photos like that had a reality all their own, or so her deepest instincts told her; there was something ancient, mythical, fabulous, and unreal about them. Many pictures had been put away because they had fallen to the floor, their glass shattered, during one of the bombings back in Berlin. One particular bombing Ingeborg remembered with clarity because a bus had overturned in the street not thirty feet from their door; it lit up the neighborhood far into the night with tall flames.

Certainly, Ingeborg never questioned her mother's wisdom in moving the three of them from Berlin into the doctor's house in Potsdam. In such matters, she was very trustful of her mother's judgment. That came partly from the fact that other people always seemed to respect Ursula's word and advice. There was something very reassuring in that. Because of it, Ingeborg could sit by the window overlooking Herr Welt's back yard and read her books without suffering a really debilitating anxiety. When she reflected on the talk of the hard, frightening winter to come, she put it from her mind. Her mother would know what to do.

There was only one matter in which Ingeborg questioned the soundness of her mother's views, and that had to do with the fate and present circumstances of her father. Ingeborg naturally remembered him well. Her last impression of him was very vivid. It was the day more than a year ago when Ursula had taken Ingeborg and Andreas on the S-Bahn train to Berlin. Her father's unit was passing through the capital from Mecklenburg, and they met on the platform. It was a very noisy, smoky, and boisterous scene. There were soldiers everywhere. There must have been two thousand. They were all talking and smoking. They had heavy bags at their feet. The shouting and talking and laughter kept up a roar, like something from nature, like a storm that went on and on. She could barely hear her father when he spoke. There were two other soldiers with him; they were fellow members of her father's signals unit. Both were much younger than he. The two of them stood back politely, at a respectful distance, as Walter said goodbye to Ursula, Ingeborg, and Andreas. Unlike other children, Ingeborg did not react with pride at the sight of her father in his uniform. To her, the uniform summoned unhappy thoughts. It signified sad leave-takings, followed by impossibly long absences. She remembered him taking her one Sunday to a dog show in the park. She would have been five or six. He was wearing his eggshell-colored corduroy jacket, with a dark tie and white shirt, and explained to her the names of all the kinds of dogs on parade by the bandstand, the poodles and schnauzers and schipperkes.

That was how she liked him to look, even though that day, airy and sun-filled, was forever ago.

Maybe it was because the Stettin Station in Berlin was so crowded, or because Ursula and Walter were talking hurriedly, animatedly, but in either case Ingeborg maintained a decorous reserve. When it came time at last for Walter Maas to embark on the troop train, Ursula began to show tears, so Andreas began also to cry. Ingeborg stood back a step, with her feet together and her skinny legs touching, yielding the space in front of herself to Andreas, whom they all still called the "baby." But Walter, in the last seconds, was looking at Ingeborg now, and there appeared a special kind of anguish in his face, as he came past Ursula and Andreas to lean and put his arms around Ingeborg. It caused her to suspect, or at least wonder at that moment, if she wasn't perhaps his favorite of all. She noticed, oddly, in the split second while kissing his cheek, the growth of tiny orange-red hairs that grew in a tuft in his ear, like the bristles of the art brush she used every Thursday at school.

But with the autumn coming on now, and nearly four full months having passed without a letter from her father, or any official word whatever of what had happened, Ingeborg had a very special dread. It accompanied her wherever she went. It was like an actual new organ that had developed inside her and secreted constantly a vaporous and sickening substance. What was worse, she knew (certainly by now, toward the start of October) that her mother had begun to lose hope. She used to say, "We'll hear something any day now." That was how she phrased it during the summer. But gradually, Ursula had yielded to a darker point of view. "Nothing is impossible." Once, too, her mother had given way to a sudden unexpected outburst of crying that frightened Ingeborg. It happened on a Sunday evening while Ingeborg was explaining to her how the figure of a bird which she had cut with scissors from the blue flyleaf of a book, a bird with spread wings, was part of a gift card that she was making to give to her father when he came back. It was from that moment, Ingeborg later realized, at the sight of her mother breaking down in the face of her worst fears, that her own resistance to any such terrifying future possibilities first took form.

One wet afternoon during this same season, in the early fall of '44, when Ingeborg was coming in at the front door of the house, she was met by Annaliese Falke, the sister of the army doctor who owned the house — and, again, toward whom Ingeborg always felt constrained to be so scrupulously well mannered. She knew as a fact by now that the small wage that her mother earned in her six-hour-a-day job in the offices of a printer in the Old Market was barely enough to meet their needs and pay for their room upstairs. In her heart, Ingeborg resented the woman. It rankled inside her. She resented having to be so painfully polite. In truth, she thought the woman strange. Whenever they all were compelled to go into the cellar during air raid alerts, the doctor's sister sat on a chair noticeably removed from the others. Annaliese Falke was an unmarried woman in her late thirties, rather bony, who wore her hair pulled back, and was always to be seen in a plain formless dress that hung like a cheap shroud from her shoulders. She had a dry disposition, too, which communicated a feeling of aloof superiority.

On this wet afternoon, Fräulein Falke led Ingeborg into the doctor's parlor. As Ingeborg had never seen what was behind the big white door in the front hall, she was pleased to discover within a very tastefully furnished chamber. She was reminded at once of their own living room in Berlin; in fact, the doctor's parlor was more imposing in every way. There was a big cretonne-covered sofa by the windows, tapestried armchairs, a shiny mahogany center table, and a Persian carpet that served to hold together and organize all the furnishings. Ingeborg took note of the rich-looking window draperies. The afternoon rain was splashing against the windows and grew in intensity in the minutes to come. At regular intervals, the big yellow streetcars moved past, under the overhanging trees on Charlottenstrasse. At this hour they often went by in tandem.

"We've never spoken," said Annaliese, showing Ingeborg just the crack of a tiny, painful smile, as she shut the door soundlessly behind her. She showed Ingeborg where to sit, pointing with the reading glasses that dangled on a black ribbon from a pin close to her throat. "I often wonder," she added, in a pleasant tone, "how you manage to be so quiet. You come and go on the stairs like a virtual ghost."

Annaliese sat down then on a hardwood settee, folded her hands, and, as before, offered the girl upstairs a faint, dusty smile. Ingeborg was at a loss for words, as she could not perceive the woman's reason for intercepting her at the door and bringing her into her parlor. Behind the sofa on which Ingeborg was sitting, the rain pelted the windows; the windowpanes, crisscrossed with strips of tape to protect against concussive bomb blasts, were fogging up with condensation.

At length, Ingeborg found her voice. She presented a prim picture. "My mother likes us to be quiet."

"And wasn't my mother the same," returned the other. "I was the eldest, and was required much of the time to look after my brother and sister. As in your case," she added, with her thin smile, "my brother was younger."

Ingeborg searched her mind for a response to that, but found nothing to say. She had taken off her coat, which was a size or two too small for her this year, and held it folded on her lap. She sat very straight and stiff on the edge of the sofa cushion, her feet together, her arms at her sides, her hair falling in a long blond sash down her back. She wanted to tell Fräulein Falke that she had once lived in a pretty house just like this one, but couldn't bring herself to say it. While Ingeborg Maas was very precocious, and generally quite capable of making interesting conversation with adults, she sensed something amiss in the doctor's sister, who looked stranger than usual. This impression gathered force in the twenty minutes to follow, as when Annaliese took a photograph album from inside the mahogany piano bench and, sitting beside Ingeborg on the sofa, leafed through the pages, pointing out who was who in the old sepia-tinted pictures. Ingeborg's discomfort intensified somewhat when the Falke woman fetched a hairbrush, insisted that Ingeborg sit round the other way, and began rhythmically to brush Ingeborg's hair in long, smooth strokes. At the moment, Ingeborg was thinking about her shoes and her feet. There were red sores on the backs of her heels from her shoes, which were too tight for her. Ursula had the ration coupons to buy shoes, but there were no shoes anywhere to be bought. In the meanwhile, Ingeborg was not enjoying Fräulein Falke's ministrations. She disliked the woman, perhaps even feared her somewhat.

"He was not an ill-behaved boy," Annaliese was saying of her doctor brother, "but like all such tykes, he could be a terror when he wanted to be."

During this perplexing interlude, while her hair was being brushed, Ingeborg reflected that her mother had probably been right in her view that they should slit open the backs of her shoes. They were the only shoes she had, and all summer long she had resisted taking that drastic measure. As always, she thought, her mother was right. If she had let Ursula open the backs of her shoes weeks ago, she would not have developed these painful sores that sometimes caused her to wince while walking.

Later that evening, after darkness had fallen, the mystery of Fräulein Falke's peculiar behavior became clear. Several people had arrived downstairs. Talking and crying could be heard, and then someone, probably Annaliese, actually wailed. Ursula, Ingeborg's mother, correctly interpreted the reason. Early in the day, hours before Annaliese accosted Ingeborg at the front door, a postal communiqué had arrived notifying the family that Dr. Falke had been killed in action. This piece of news struck Ingeborg a hard blow, coming at a time when she was struggling in secret to overcome fears about her father. In the past several days, the attempt to sustain her faith had become an earnest undertaking. The more she thought about it — such as this morning, in school, when Frau Redeker was leading the class in the singing of "Let Us Gather Together to Pray" — the more certain she grew of his safety. She was standing behind the new girl in class, Ingrid, and was singing along with all the others, but she was also looking back into a secret part of her mind where her father sometimes appeared. Usually she saw him as he was on that day on the railway platform, when he came forward to kiss her goodbye, and there was that anguish in his face. This morning, it was different. He was elsewhere. He was coming along a country road on foot. Walking beside him was one of the boys from the Stettin Station. Their army coats were open. There was a row of poplar trees. The sun was shining through them. She was singing along with the others in class, while watching him on the road.

Tonight, in the middle of the evening, after they had gone to bed, the air raid sirens began to howl; but because of the grief below, Ursula said they would not take shelter in the cellar unless they actually heard bombing nearby. Often, the big Allied air formations heading for Berlin passed directly overhead with a profound ghastly roar that set everything shaking, and the sky would light up as the antiaircraft gunners in and around Potsdam opened fire. Minutes later, when bombing did commence over Berlin, as far as twenty miles away entire buildings were set shaking. A year ago, a formation of forty or fifty enemy bombers was thought to be a major raid; by now, however, there were sometimes a thousand or more planes. They came on and on for an hour or more, in an endless train; and everything trembled. But tonight, Ingeborg was almost relieved to hear the sirens because she had been lying awake in bed with nothing to think about except how news kept coming of people who had been killed. Helga Dorn's brother was killed at Normandy; two of her classmates had lost their fathers; and now it was the man downstairs in whose house they lived.

Ursula spoke up to say that the planes were passing somewhere to the north. The sound of the flak was more subdued than usual, as were the reverberations coming from the attack itself. Ingeborg was looking at the wall, with her back to the windows. The floor and walls vibrated, as they always did. She was trying not to think about the doctor's sister downstairs.

"Andreas is actually sleeping," said Ursula from the darkness behind, marveling over the boy's capacity to slumber during raids.

"I hope," said Ingeborg, in that scolding voice she often used when referring to her brother, "that he's not sucking his thumb."

Sighing, Ursula replied with maternal indulgence. "There are worse things than sucking one's thumb."

"Then he *is*," said Ingeborg, "sucking his thumb."

Ingeborg could be a stickler sometimes.

One of the most pleasant days early that fall, as far as Ingeborg was concerned, was the Sunday afternoon when Ursula Maas took her daughter out to the village of Glindowsee to visit an old friend. It was a two- or three-hour walk into the country. Edda, the friend, along with her husband, Otto, had just moved into the vicinity and were occupying a small two-room garden house that belonged to one of the old outlying Potsdam estates close to the lake. Otto worked as a staff driver for an official at the Propaganda Ministry in Berlin. It was his employer, Count Bertold von Salmuth-Tresckow, who owned the big stucco house in Glindowsee, where Otto, it seemed, was on call at all hours.

"Edda and I," Ursula explained, with Ingeborg walking before her on the roadside, "trained together in secretarial work. That was long before the war came. It was just after that when I went to work at the book company." She teased Ingeborg. "That's why you like books so much."

Ingeborg struck an adult tone, calling to mind a phrase that her mother had once let fall. "Was that," she said, "when you were 'carrying' me?"

"Yes, it was." Ursula nodded and smiled.

From time to time, an auto or bicyclist went by on the road, and, at odd intervals, military vehicles, mostly trucks. One truck was packed full of antiaircraft gunners. Ingeborg recognized them by the insignia they wore. They were all standing up in the back and looked to be basking their faces in the noonday sunlight.

Just beyond the village, the roadway on which they were walking turned to gravel, and at the end of it there was a cast-iron gate. Through the gate loomed clearly the big stucco house. To Ingeborg's eye, it was an important-look-ing house, with a lot of chimneys, and grass all around it, a gate letting into it, and everywhere a scattering of fruit trees. Ursula took Ingeborg's hand as she pushed open the gate. Edda must have been watching for them because she appeared at once, coming down a path through the wood on their left to meet them. At the top of the path was the gar-dener's house, and fifty feet back from that, a wooden pavil-ion overlooking the lake.

Edda ran the last few steps, clasping Ursula about the waist, squeezing her, and kissing her on both cheeks, a demonstration that Ingeborg thought excessive, although she did like Edda's looks. She also liked the looks of the small gardener's house into which Edda and Otto had re-cently moved. With its gingerbread trim and prettily shaped windows, it was like a house in a storybook. There were only two rooms, quite sizable, one above the other, with a narrow staircase connecting them. There was a fireplace with plates and pictures on the mantel, summer-type fur-nishings, hand-tied carpets, and a window seat built into the wall that faced the villa. Ingeborg went to the settee and looked out at the big house with its chimneys outlined against the sky. Sudden breezes blew the dry fruit tree leaves into the air in sudden spiraling gusts, or sent them racing low across the grass in the direction of the house.

Ursula opened the parcel she had brought with her and set it on the table. It contained some bread, Ingeborg's book, two potatoes, some Harz cheese, and a half bottle of wine which she had bartered from a coworker. Acquiring even minimal rations was by now a daily trial.

"I don't think we'll be living here much longer," Edda was in the midst of saying. "I've been ordered to report to the nearest Manpower board. Part of the 'Total War' proclamation!" she exclaimed cynically, and made a face. "The only work available for me out here would be in the Young Women's Compulsory Rural Service. I would be milking cows. I don't think I've ever even seen a cow!"

Ingeborg sat on the window seat, listening to them.

Ursula sympathized with her friend. "I certainly would not know how to milk a cow."

"Ingeborg," Edda called playfully across the room to her. "Can you milk a cow?"

In replying, Ingeborg gave her mother's friend a sample of her theatricality. "I shall not milk a cow," she said, "if I live to be a hundred."

Both Edda and Ursula reacted gaily at the dramatic picture that Ingeborg presented of the prim, sober-faced child who saw herself as superior to farmyard chores.

"Why don't you go to the Manpower Board in Potsdam?" Ursula inquired of her friend.

"For me to work in Potsdam would require two hours of bicycling each day, just to get back and forth, in all kinds of weather, and that with winter coming. I don't know what to do, darling. In Berlin, the bombings go on now day and night. Otto and I were at the ends of our wits. At the Zoo station, I saw a young man, who had lost one of his legs at the front and who works there as a porter, throw himself on the basement floor during a daylight raid. He was squirming about and moaning, 'I can't take it anymore!' It's gotten so bad. And just to leave Berlin now, even for a day, you have to have a special pass."

Here, Ursula signified with her eyes that this subject was not appropriate in the presence of her daughter. Before preparing lunch, Edda took the two of them outdoors on a long walk in search of mushrooms. They kept to the high ground above the lake. The yellowed leaves on the boughs overhead and covering the earth before them lighted up from time to time as the sunlight came and went. After about an hour, as they turned and came traipsing back along the shorefront of the lake, Ingeborg noticed that not a single mention had been made of her father; a lapse that convinced her that both Edda and her mother were losing faith in his safety. Ingeborg looked out to the lake, where a light wind was corrugating the surface of the water. When the sun shone, she could see the yellow of the trees on the opposite shore reflected on the waters of the lake.

Coming up toward the pavilion, Edda complimented her old friend on the attractions of her daughter. Ursula colored with pride and ran a smoothing hand over Ingeborg's head. "Ingeborg is my strength," she said lovingly.

"She's very thoughtful," Edda said with admiration. "Very pensive. Very pretty, too. She seems very advanced."

"She takes care of Andreas when I can't be at home, and does her schoolwork. She even brings up water from the pump."

"*And* I can iron," Ingeborg pointed out, with her lips pinched.

"She knows how to iron!" Ursula brightened happily over the girl's egoism. "She stands in place for me in queues at the food shop and never complains. She helps in a hundred ways. She's my little hero."

"Have you made any plans," Edda went on, thoughtlessly, "to try to get west of here, if worst comes to worst?"

Ursula shot Edda a forbidding look for having broached once more a topic that was altogether taboo and very dangerous besides to indulge: the idea of avoiding at all costs staying in the path of the advancing Russian armies, when that time should come. Ursula was simpler than Edda in worldly matters, and was also perhaps more trusting in Providence and in the ability of the German nation to protect its own. She answered Edda's question, nonetheless. "We will be happy to stay here in Potsdam," she said, "now and after the war."

In the next second, to Ursula's regret at the turn in their conversation, Ingeborg piped up in a reflexive manner. "If we didn't stay, my father wouldn't know where to find us."

Before the words left her mouth, Ingeborg wished she had not said them. A look of alarm passed through her face. She had violated her own first injunction. She was right, also, in her anticipation that such a blunder would produce looks of discomfort on their faces. Edda glanced away. Ursula leaned instinctively to kiss Ingeborg on the temples, but Ingeborg recoiled inwardly from her mother's love. She gave Ursula a steely blue stare that spoke worlds.

At the table, later on, Ingeborg forgot about her resentment and watched with interest and pleasure as the two women worked painstakingly to prepare their meal. Ursula spoke openly about her concerns for the undernourishment of the children and said how lucky she was to have be-friended someone at work who gave her a bottle of milk now and then. In the past year, the small ration for jam, butter, cheese, vegetables, and such, had been halved, to by now less than subsistence levels. Meat, of course, was scarcer still.

"In that way," Edda was explaining, "it's a little better to be out in the country. People manage to find other foods."

Ingeborg was enjoying the aroma in the room, as her mother and Edda went about the business of preparing a sauce, potato dumplings, and a fragrant soup. Otto had ac-quired some pieces of chicken from his employer's cook, which delicacies Edda added to the pot. Ursula had taught Ingeborg excellent table manners, and when her bowl was placed before her, Ingeborg, sitting very straight, took up her spoon, leaned forward a fraction, and addressed her meal with conspicuous dignity. Ever since that moment out-doors, when Ingeborg had drawn back from her mother's so-licitous kiss, Ursula kept glancing worriedly at her, stealing surreptitious peeks. But Ingeborg revealed no visible clue whatever of a lingering reaction, as she reached and dipped her spoon just so into her steaming soup.

As luck would have it, when Ingeborg went outdoors by herself after lunch, she saw the lady who owned the stucco house strolling idly down the grassy roadway from the back door. In nearly the same moment, the lady glanced up to-ward the gardener's cottage and spotted the figure of the blond ten-year-old standing among the trees. She waved to Ingeborg. Ingeborg reflected just for a second, then waved her hand in return. Within two or three minutes, the two of them were walking and visiting together under the fruit trees on the lawn that ran uphill from the iron gate to the house.

"You looked like a little wood sprite standing up there," said the lady. "I thought I was seeing things."

Ingeborg explained presently that her mother and Edda Holtzman were friends from years ago in Berlin. "I was born in Berlin," she added.

"And you live in Potsdam now?"

"We live in a room on Charlottenstrasse."

"I see." The lady treated Ingeborg's every word with considered seriousness.

Ingeborg walked at her side. She noticed in passing that the fruit trees had been picked clean. There was only an occasional stunted or rotten apple underfoot. Mostly, she stole glances at the lady, whom she guessed was about the same age as her mother, which was thirty-five. The lady was tallish and very pleasant to look at. She had high cheekbones, a delicate throat, and pale skin and hair. Taken in all, she looked very important. That was what Ingeborg liked best about her. She was sure that this was the lady who owned the house, and that it was she and her husband whom Otto drove back and forth to Berlin. Her husband worked at a ministry, Edda had said. Ingeborg didn't know what a ministry was, but pictured in her mind a domed churchlike building with flags outside it. She remembered a building on Hardenbergstrasse, near which they had once lived. It was called a courthouse. She could not remember seeing anyone go in or out of it, but imagined a ministry to look like that.

While stepping along in the grass, Ingeborg suddenly recalled the unsightly condition of the backs of her shoes. Several days earlier, her mother had made a vertical slit in each, to make them comfortable. From that moment, Ingeborg made sure not to walk in front of the woman, who could not help but notice how ugly they were. When the lady asked Ingeborg her name, she responded in full. They were in the middle of the lawn by now. The lady's hair shone in the sun.

"My name is Ingeborg Maas."

"Ingeborg!" The lady slowed in her walking, in the way of expressing surprise. "That's always been one of my favorite names."

For a moment or so, Ingeborg lost her studied reserve; she colored to the roots of her hair. Feeling the heat rising in her temples, she looked down at the ground in embarrassment. She had always believed her name to be lovelier than others, but no one else had ever noticed.

"I knew a beautiful Norwegian singer who was called Ingeborg. She sang in the church choir. Her voice was thrilling." The lady leaned in confidence and dropped her voice. "She was not nearly as pretty as you."

Perhaps for the last time in her life Ingeborg betrayed an infantile expression, as her lips twisted in a distorted expression of shyness and vanity. She kept her eyes down.

"But from now on," said the other, "whenever I hear the name Ingeborg, I shall always think of you."

Ingeborg never understood quite how it came to pass, but not twenty minutes later, the lady had gone indoors and come out again, and put Ingeborg in possession of a very pretty pair of black shoes that looked almost like dancing slippers. They were not perfectly new, but they shone like anthracite. "Those you can grow into, if they're too big."

"They're not too big." Thrilled with her new shoes, Ingeborg glanced over instinctively toward the trees and the gardener's house in anticipation of showing them to her mother. She held them side by side before her.

"They belonged to my younger sister, Sigi, who never

throws anything away, even when it gets too small. Those were the shoes that she wore as a young girl to my wedding. If I had others, I would give them to you. To tell the truth, Ingeborg, I don't have much of anything, except a bunch of coupons and ration cards."

"My mother has clothing coupons," said Ingeborg, conscious of the need to contribute to their conversation, "but there is nothing to buy."

"Well, we were both lucky today. You got Sigi's patent leather shoes, and I got a half hour of your lovely company, one of the very few pleasures that I've had in weeks."

Ingeborg strove to prolong their talk. "Were you married in a big church?" she asked.

As they started back down the lawn, the lady rested a hand on Ingeborg's shoulder. "Indeed, it was quite big. I was married in the Frauenkirche, in Munich. That has always been my favorite church. When you're grown up, maybe you'll visit it."

"I will." Ingeborg continued to carry the shoes in both hands, like something consecrated and inviolable.

"And when you do, you will remember me?"

"Oh, yes." Ingeborg was more than earnest on that point.

The leaves skittering past made a dry rustling sound and blew away into the woods in a sudden yellow gust. They were approaching the path to the gardener's house when Ingeborg asked the woman her name.

"My name is hard to remember. Of course," she added, playfully, "*I* can remember it easily enough. It's Berenice von Salmuth-Tresckow. Do you like that name?"

"Yes, I do." Ingeborg appeared momentarily concentrated, as she pronounced the name silently to herself.

Before parting, the lady sought to learn the fate or whereabouts of the ten-year-old's father. "Will you move back to Berlin after the war?" she asked.

"I don't know what my father will say, but I think we will. Our house is much too small. We lived in a very nice house in Berlin, on Fasanenstrasse. My father is a printer."

Ingeborg was getting more talkative by the minute. This was what she liked to do; she liked to put her capabilities on parade. It was her chief way of making herself attractive to others. She also liked looking up at the face of the von Salmuth-Tresckow lady. Her cheekbones and forehead were luminous as a seashell, and she had gray-blue eyes, a little bit like the color of the lake water when you could see the sky in it.

"Someday," said Ingeborg, "I would like to be a bookseller. My father suggested that to me once. He said we could do it together." Ingeborg was stretching the truth somewhat, but in fact she couldn't remember exactly what he had said.

"I think you would be wonderful at that."

"I like books."

"I'm sure you do."

"I like books better than anything else." For a rare moment, Ingeborg was able to talk comfortably about her father; and she realized only now how painful and unpleasant it was to have to keep him as a secret. "I always get books for gifts. I have dozens of them under my bed, a lot of them from my father, especially my first ones, the little children's books."

"You've read them all, Ingeborg?"

"Some of them I have read five or six times. I read two or three books a week."

Ingeborg did not notice that the lady was regarding her

with a very tender expression, as they reached the gate and the foot of the path leading up to the cottage.

"My favorite books are romances about knights and ladies. I am reading a book by Sir Walter Scott."

"And you say you're only ten?"

Ingeborg answered objectively. "I read a lot of books that older children can't read."

"I think your father's idea about bookselling is just right for you."

"That's what we want to do," she said.

"Just think about it. You would be surrounded with books. You would have all the books you want."

"And my father," said Ingeborg, completing the picture of a blissful future.

"Of course." They had paused at the edge of the woods. "Where is your father?" she asked. "Is he in Potsdam?"

"My father is in Russia," said Ingeborg.

At that, the lady looked off to the hill where the wind was ripping leaves from the birches. "I see," she replied quietly.

As it happened, Ingeborg was befriended that autumn by yet another rather illustrious figure, this time in the person of a fourteen-year-old girl named Beatrice von Stutterheim who attended Ingeborg's school. Ingeborg knew her by sight and, like many other students, was very admiring of the older girl's looks and ways. The girl was known as Betka to her schoolmates and was said to be descended from an old and distinguished East Prussian family. Part of her popularity stemmed from the signs she gave of an independent, even rebellious spirit. It was Betka who was sharply reprimanded at school for having been seen wearing a pale lipstick on Saturday evening at Vespers service. The following Saturday, the headstrong girl made a point of repeating the offense. On the second occasion, Ursula and her children were present in the nave of St. Nicholas's. Ingeborg saw Betka enter the magnificent church and take her place in a pew. She leaned and whispered to her mother. That, she said, was Betka, and she *was* wearing lipstick again. Ursula smiled at the look of wonder and suspense in Ingeborg's face and admonished her please to keep quiet.

It was never clear how this latest act of self-assertion might have worked out, however, as within ten minutes of the opening of the service, sirens sounded the air raid warning, and everyone trooped downstairs. On this night, the big air formation bound for Berlin came directly overhead. The flak was heavy, but muffled appreciably by the deep stone foundations of the historic church. Here and there, in the cellar of the church, shone the pale glow of candles, like the light of distant planets. A man with a walrus mustache, sitting nearby, identified the bombers as American. He could distinguish aircraft just by their sound, he said. He talked without letup, until three older women, who were knitting, turned on him angrily and told him to keep his tongue. It was bad enough, said one of them, to be trapped in an icy cellar half the night, "without having a radio announcer next door."

For more than two hours, the earth shook from the constant explosions taking place in Berlin. The picture of the worshippers in the vast cellar took on the aspect of a dream, hunched quietly in their chairs, some swaying with sleep. Andreas was in Ursula's lap, fitfully waking and sleeping, while Ingeborg leaned drowsily against her mother's arm. Someone nearby could be heard during a lull humming what sounded to Ingeborg like a requiem she had heard on Monday-night radio, when, suddenly, from close by, in the direction of Burgstrasse, came a deafening explosion that shook the church to its foundations. People cried out instinctively. Several jumped to their feet. At the same time, all the candles tipped over and flickered out. A second explosion created a shock wave that felt to Ingeborg as if someone had pounded her ears with both fists. She grabbed hold of her mother in the dark. Everything was shaking in a frightening way. The sound of a door blowing in was accompanied by a rush of cold air, and five or six detonations followed in rapid sequence, the bombs whizzing down into the streets nearby. The flak increased in intensity, producing its own concussive effects. From the floor above could be heard the rumble of pews and furnishings skidding about, and the constant sound of glass breaking.

Ursula and her children were by this time veterans of air raids, although the explosions tonight were very near at hand. When they emerged from the church, after the all-clear sounded, an hour or more before midnight, all were surprised to find the streets and rooftops layered with snow, the first of the year. The snow came spinning down in thick, wet flakes and obscured from view the flames of several fires. In the Old Market, not a hundred yards away, a bus and three or four automobiles lay smashed and jumbled in the street. Bomb craters pitted the roadway in front of the Rathaus. Firemen and rescue workers were toiling furiously amid the burning ruins of what had been a three-story house just west of Kaiserstrasse, by the Kanal. Their silhouettes seen through the blur of the snow and against the backdrop of a curtain of fire formed an infernal picture. Ursula carried Andreas, while tugging Ingeborg by the hand, the three of them going home as expeditiously as possible. The air was heavy with smoke and the smell of gas fumes. A black pall belched forth now and again in the direction of Charlottenstrasse. Ingeborg's heart was beating like mad because she could feel the cold dread in the pressure of her mother's hand and in the urgency of her movements, the fear that their own house would be a smoking ruins. Turning at last into Charlottenstrasse, and spotting their house, with the snow on the sills and stoop, her mother spoke her relief aloud. "Thank God," she said.

Around midnight, after Andreas had gone to sleep, Ingeborg's mother used up one of her carefully hoarded candles, just to sit up for a little while with Ingeborg and talk. The electric power was out in the district, and perhaps in all of Potsdam, so far as one could tell. By this time, toward the close of 1944, the shortages of fuel and food were acute. Ursula had draped the windows to retain what heat there was, and on this night expended a small quantity of coal in the old-fashioned porcelain stove. There was kindling in a pile by the door. Ingeborg guessed shrewdly that her mother had been more anxious than usual and wanted the two of them to have a pleasant visit. These were the cozy moments that Ingeborg liked best. Sometimes her mother would talk about her very early girlhood days, or describe how shy Ingeborg's father had been when they met at a dance in Berlin, and how she, Ursula, had had to go across the room to him and initiate a conversation, and how speechless he was, and the look of helplessness on his face, and, best of all, how she had loved him at first sight. (Ingeborg remembered the exact words her mother had used in one such description of the meeting. "The minute I saw him," she said, "I loved him to distraction.")

"I hope," Ingeborg had said on that occasion, in her prim-
mest manner, "that you didn't chase after him, Mommy."

"I didn't have to," said Ursula. "The next day, at five o'-
clock, he was standing outside the little building where I
worked, by the corner mailbox."

"He was afraid of you, Mommy?"

"I wouldn't call it that," said Ursula. "He was very young,
and he had no sisters at home, and was somewhat afraid of
girls. He was just not sure of himself in that way. He didn't
know quite what to do after the night we met. So he just
came to the street where I worked, and stood out there, and
waited."

"You were pleased, Mommy?"

"I tried not to show it. But I'll never forget the sight of
him, in his navy blue suit and a funny yellow necktie, just
standing out there, looking like something that had been hit
by lightning."

Ingeborg thrilled to the picture of her father, with his long
sorrowful face, standing at the mailbox, tongue-tied, as her
mother came into the street and discovered him there. "After that, it was better?"

"In no time, we were famous friends. We met after work
almost every day. I sent him a holiday card one day that first
month, and said in it that my heart jumped every time I saw
him coming. That same day, barely one hour after I mailed
the card, he said that very same thing to me. It was such a
coincidental thing to hear. 'When I see you coming toward
me in the street,' he said, 'my heart jumps!' Same words, exactly. Same day. Almost within the hour." Ursula's voice,
grown soft, conveyed the mystery of it all.

These were the stories that Ingeborg lived to hear. On this
night, however, while stirring the fire, as rescue vehicles

rattled past on the cobbles below, Ursula surrendered to darker concerns. She was wearing a big sweater and stood at the stove with her back to Ingeborg. "I don't want everything taken away from me," she said.

While Ingeborg was washing her face of the sooty smoke from the air outdoors with a damp washcloth, Ursula reheated a pot of weak, rather strange-tasting tea, and cut a small piece of bread into four slices.

"I wish it was Monday," said Ingeborg, "so we could listen to the Berlin orchestra on the radio."

"Without electricity, we won't be listening to anything on the radio, will we?"

Here Ingeborg catalogued her favorite pleasures. "I like the philharmonic on Mondays, I like the band we hear sometimes in the palace park, and I like the stories you tell."

"And your schoolwork and books," Ursula added.

"The best hour at school is when we talk about the stories we've read. Friday afternoon, Frau Redeker sent me upstairs to a class with older students because she said I read better than anyone else my age."

"Who is the teacher upstairs?"

"Herr Geissler."

"Is he the elderly man who wears a long black coat and a black hat with an immense brim?"

Ingeborg laughed instantly. "There's a boy in the upstairs class named Hansi Heiss. He said that when Herr Geissler stands still by the front door of the school he looks like a tall black toadstool."

Ursula tried not to laugh over the comic depiction, as it seemed disrespectful. "He's very elderly," she said.

"He's ancient, Mommy." Ingeborg made a face upon tasting the tea. "He's a hundred years old."

"Ingeborg, please." Ursula joined her daughter at the table.

Remembering something, Ingeborg laughed suddenly, and set down her cup. "Hansi's brother said that Herr Geissler died ten years ago, but keeps walking around because no one has told him yet."

This time, Ursula could not suppress her amusement. She was pleased and delighted, as well, with the picture of her sophisticated child holding forth in the glow of the candle. The stove next to them was putting out a little heat.

"My left side is nice and warm," said Ingeborg, "but my right side is cold."

"We'll change sides in a minute."

Time and again, from outdoors, came the sound of vehicles hurrying past, bumping along noisily, tires squealing at the street corner. The firefighting and rescue operations continued for hours. Twice, the lights came on and immediately went out again. Ingeborg and her mother were wearing heavy sweaters and had draped blankets over their knees, as the floor was cold and drafty. While Ingeborg chatted away, entertaining her mother, they switched sides at the table. Peeking outdoors, Ingeborg beheld an unusual sight. One of the big yellow trams, two cars moving in tandem, both empty and fully lighted, went by soundlessly in the snow. There was power in the streetcar lines. It was a bit eerie to see a tram running so late at night on Charlottenstrasse. Now and again, it threw a blue spark. The branches of the trees lining the cobbled street were etched with snow. Ingeborg shut the draperies.

"I think," Ursula was saying, "that Hansi and his brother are very clever boys who enjoy teasing people."

"Hansi's brother is called Bübchen. He came home on leave for bravery. Did you know that soldiers get special leave for bravery?"

"Yes. It does happen."

"They said that Bübchen came and visited the classroom upstairs, and Herr Geissler asked Bübchen to show Hansi and his classmates the desk that he sat at five years ago, in that same room."

"That was a very thoughtful thing to do," said Ursula. "Very inspiring, I suspect."

Ingeborg laughed. "A girl named Melanie Wipperfurth said that the girls in the class were more inspired than the boys, because Bübchen, she said, is beautiful to look at!"

"And this," Ursula twitted Ingeborg, "was what you all talked about during your Friday story hour in the upstairs classroom?"

"It was such fun, Mommy! Herr Geissler can't hear well at all, and thought we were all talking about the mountain climber story."

"And you were all talking about Bübchen Heiss."

"Yes! . . . Mommy," she said, as an afterthought, "I like the older children better."

"I'm not surprised."

"Did you," Ingeborg pressed her mother, "play with older children when you were ten?"

"I was not so smart as you." As she often did, Ursula reached and ran the flat of her hand smoothly over Ingeborg's blond head. "It just means that you're quicker than most."

"I know more stories."

Ursula imitated an intonation often employed by her daughter. "*And* you remember them," she said.

Ingeborg laughed over that. Her mother often teased her by copycatting the way she spoke, which, she had been told, betrayed her vanity.

"I'd like to write a story sometime about a very old teacher who wears black clothing and a big black hat and doesn't know that he died years ago because no one had told him."

"That's enough, Ingeborg. It's unkind to make fun of someone who should really be honored and revered for what he does. Herr Geissler is taking the place of a much younger person, I'm sure, who was mobilized and called away."

"That's what I would write." Ingeborg was not especially susceptible to her mother's gentle remonstrances. "Do you know what else Hansi said about Bübchen? He said that Bübchen told the class that Herr Geissler was the only person in Potsdam that is not a National Socialist. Do you know why?"

"I don't want to hear this sort of story!"

"Bübchen said that the only people that were not National Socialists were people who had been deaf for years."

"This Bübchen is hearing such things from others, and they are not funny, and it can be even dangerous to talk like that."

"Hansi said that everyone laughed, and Herr Geissler laughed, too."

Ursula said no more. She could picture the handsome young soldier, with his smart uniform and his Iron Cross, entertaining the thirteen-year-olds, while the antique schoolmaster smiled and laughed along.

"Bübchen is in Holland," Ingeborg said. "I hope next time he comes home he will visit the class again. Especially on a

Friday, when I am allowed to go upstairs. How far away is Holland, Mommy?"

"Quite far."

"How far?"

"Maybe —" Ursula didn't know. "Maybe three hundred miles," she said.

Ingeborg had noticed in recent weeks that certain words and expressions had mysteriously vanished from her mother's vocabulary. Far and away, the most conspicuous of these words was "Russia." Ingeborg, too, had stopped saying it. They used to talk about it quite a lot. She remembered her mother telling her once that the hour was always later in Russia. In the afternoon, when she came out of school, it was already dusk in the east. Sometimes when they sat listening to the radio in the evening, she could picture her father asleep in the middle of the night, nestled under his blankets. Somehow he seemed safer to her that way. Her father was called a field radioman. Sometimes, at moments like this, when he came unbidden among her thoughts, she wondered if he wasn't transmitting himself to her across the wintry distances, on his radio.

When Ursula looked across in the glow of the candle, Ingeborg had her eyes down. She was toying with the crust of her bread. She was absorbed in her thoughts of field radios and time zones. She looked unhappy. What she did not know was that three weeks earlier her mother had got back in the mail a packet of the last five letters that she had written to Walter. The earliest of the five was dated August 2, almost four months ago. Three written inquiries to the Army High Command in Berlin had produced no response. In fact, the east had become a boiling cauldron. Technically, there was no longer a Russian front. The

Russian armies had already pushed their way up to the Vistula, in Poland.

Diagonally across the street from where she lived stood one of the oldest houses in Potsdam, a three-storied, smoke-blackened edifice that had served for ages as a church rectory. The church to which it belonged, which was located two streets away, had been pulverized months ago. It was a ruin, just one wall standing with gaping window openings. The rector and his family, with no church to administer nor a flock to oversee, had betaken themselves away to the rector's home village in Pomerania. But in the week following the raid, something took place at the big house across the way that produced a tantalizing effect on Ingeborg's romantic imagination.

Returning home from school, Ingeborg came upon a horse-pulled van parked outside the rectory. Two workmen were busy unloading furnishings, bearing packing cases and such up the stairs through the open front door. Far more compelling, though, was the sight of the adolescent girl who was standing on the stair top, whom Ingeborg recognized at once. The girl was reading a letter. The pages fluttering in her fingers appeared transparent in the sunlight. It was the girl whom all of the older children talked about, the headstrong individual who had twice worn makeup to Saturday night Vespers. She was Betka von Stutterheim.

As Ingeborg came along the walk, the girl glanced up, waved the pages of her letter in greeting, and smiled. To Ingeborg's own surprise, she waved back. Heart thumping, Ingeborg made her way around the steaming horse, and beveled out into the street. Crossing the tram tracks and snowy cobblestones, she endeavored to keep her shoulders and head straight, stepping along with conscious dignity. At her door, she longed to look back, but thought it undignified to do so and let herself into the house. In Ingeborg's mind, the slender, dark-haired von Stutterheim girl standing on the rectory steps was a figure of mythic derivation, like a heroine in one of her books. Ingeborg was so imbued with feelings of romantic excitement that she walked right past Annaliese Falke in the foyer without so much as a glance or word of greeting and climbed the front stairs.

The perception that the von Stutterheim girl and her family had moved into the venerable old house across the street was erroneous in part; the girl was living that year in the household of Dieter and Anna Freytag, a man and woman who had been employed for years as servants of the girl's parents, and who looked after her needs. Dieter Freytag served also those days as a civilian employee at the Potsdam Military School, a minor bureaucrat who spent hours every day filling out supply requisition schedules. It was Dieter, though, who was entrusted with the responsibility of maintaining everyday moral authority over the high-spirited girl living in his house, a duty that he sweated and strove earnestly to fulfill.

That first night, Ingeborg peeked out many times through the draperies. Electric power had been restored, and she was curious to see which upstairs room of the old rectory would be illuminated. While their meatless supper that evening consisted of nothing more tasteful or nutritious than red cabbage soup and bread, Ingeborg was too preoccupied to notice. In the days that followed, she tried several times to put herself in the way of her magnificent neighbor. The girl they called Betka was in and out of her thoughts from morning to night. If nothing else, this obsession gave her relief, especially in the nighttime, from agonizing over another day having passed with no letter from her father.

As matters evolved, great inventiveness was not required of Ingeborg in her acquainting herself with Beatrice von Stutterheim. On Saturday afternoon, while returning home from the bakery on Brandenburgerstrassse, someone called hello to her. Ingeborg turned, and there coming rapidly behind her on the sidewalk was the girl herself. She walked in a brisk athletic way and smiled often and spontaneously.

"My new neighbor," she said.

"I saw you moving in." Ingeborg's face turned pink.

"Yes, I know. You're the girl with the fairy-tale hair and the pretty purple coat." Betka was very animated and walked with the loose-limbed urgency of a hiker, compelling Ingeborg to quicken her steps to keep up. "How long have you lived on Charlottenstrasse?"

Ingeborg hurried at her side. "We've lived here over two years, but before that," she added, wishing to associate herself with the great capital, "we lived in Berlin."

"Berlin?" Beatrice showed interest.

"We lived near the Zoo station."

"How lucky."

"My mother says that we are lucky not to be there."

"That's what I mean," said the von Stutterheim girl. "How lucky you were to live there once, and how lucky not to be there anymore. I've been to Berlin a few times. It's like visiting the moon."

"The moon?" Ingeborg was infatuated with the girl and strove to present her brightest side. Her thoughts were going a mile a minute.

"You know," the girl gestured, "with everything flat and

twisted out of shape. And it's smoking all the time! Did you ever see *Dr. Caligari's Cabinet*?"

Ingeborg shook her head. She couldn't match the speed of the older girl's thinking. Everything about her seemed urgent and rapid-fire.

"That's what it's like," Betka said. She laughed. "And they keep coming back and bombing it some more. There are soldiers everywhere, and no one can imagine what they're doing there because there's nothing to protect and nothing to protect it with. So they walk around in mobs, and salute one another, and go down into the U-Bahn, and come up *out* of the U-Bahn, and wherever they enter, and wherever they come out, it's exactly the same."

Ingeborg was charmed by the way the teenage girl talked to her. She was unable to put a finger on it, but she sensed something profane in the girl's reckless air.

"Do you ever go to the movies?"

"I did when I was small," said Ingeborg.

"I'll take you sometime," said Betka.

"You would?"

"But the pictures are awful. Especially the newsreels. The newsreels like to show dead bodies! Everyone in the theater is squirming in his seat." Betka laughed as before, then abruptly reached and took hold of the book Ingeborg was carrying, a translation of a Sir Walter Scott novel. "You can read this?" Betka regarded Ingeborg closely, as if she had not seen her before. She opened the volume to the bookmark. "You've almost finished it!"

"I read a hundred pages every day."

"God in heaven, do you do anything else?"

Ingeborg's heart swelled with pride, but she was speechless. She liked looking at Betka's face and eyes. She had smooth skin and dark oil-colored eyes with golden lights in them.

"I've read some of his books," Betka added. "I've read *Rob Roy* and *Ivanhoe.*"

"I've read both of those," Ingeborg admitted.

The older girl waved the book in the air vigorously. "With the tournaments and the jousting!" she exclaimed.

On impulse, Ingeborg wanted to point out that her father's name, like that of the author, was Walter, but lately had developed a deepening reluctance to broach the subject of her father in any way. It troubled her that he was becoming a secret that she kept.

The snow had melted from the trees along Charlottenstrasse and was dripping on the walkway. Ingeborg was still hurrying to keep pace, searching her mind for something to say that would help her to see the beautiful girl again. At the rectory steps, the idea flashed upon her. "Would you have any books I could borrow?" she asked.

Reaching, Betka took hold of her by the hand and pulled Ingeborg up the stairs and into the ancient house. Indoors, Ingeborg examined her surroundings. She knew at a glance that most of the furnishings had been there for years, doubtless left behind when the rector moved out, because the big front room was crowded with things from one end to the other. Much of it, like the upholstered chairs and the carpets, was old and worn. The room was quite dark, and was made only darker by virtue of the massive tables, bookcases, tall-backed chairs, and the high wainscoting that reached all about the room and converged on the big black-mouthed fireplace. Still, to Ingeborg's active sensibility, it was a very romantic setting. Their own apartment on Fasanenstrasse in Berlin, with its three pretty rooms and bright kitchen — and where she had been so happy, in the days when Andreas was a baby in his crib, and her father had sat at the table with his newspaper open before him — was inconsequential by contrast with the big dark reception parlor of the rectory.

While Betka darted upstairs to her room to get Ingeborg a book, Anna Freytag, a stoutish lady wearing a heavy woolen sweater over her dress and apron, came down the hall from the back of the house.

"Are you waiting for Betka?"

Ingeborg was standing in the late-afternoon shadows by the front door.

"Yes, I am."

The woman smiled very pleasantly. "Are you a friend of hers?"

Ingeborg stammered momentarily. "Not really," she said, unable to make such a claim. "I live across the street."

"Yes, she is!" Betka called down from the top of the stairs, and a second later came bounding down the steps. "Even if I don't know her name."

"I'm sorry!" Ingeborg exclaimed, turning to the other. "I'm Ingeborg Maas."

Betka pressed two books into Ingeborg's hands and led her jauntily out to the steps.

"I'm Betka," she said.

During these same days when Ingeborg was being befriended by her illustrious neighbor, her mother had made a change and taken a new job. She began working as a Red Cross nurse at the state hospital on Turkstrasse, where there was an acute shortage of help. Under the new Total War strictures, nearly all the male medical orderlies had been called up and ordered to the front. At the same time, the number of war-wounded mounted by the day, to the point where an impressive tent city had sprouted up on the island in the Havel just south of the Old City to accommodate the latest arrivals from the front.

For her part, Ingeborg was pleased about her mother's new position. She liked the starched uniform her mother wore, with its white apron and cap, and was not unaware that it made her mother look somehow more important in the eyes of other people, especially the lady downstairs. Despite Fräulein Falke's now attiring herself in black every day, in respect for the doctor, Ingeborg still resented the woman for her having had to smile and bow before her all these months. It had reached the point now where Ingeborg usually ignored her, partly, no doubt, too, because the grieving Annaliese had become a living reminder of Ingeborg's own deepest fears.

At the same time, Ursula secured a similar position at the hospital for her friend Edda Holtzman. Edda then also rented a room from Fräulein Falke. As a further improvement, there was always a little extra food now, brought home from the canteen at the hospital, and Edda's presence in the house and her coming and going at their upstairs door — along with her willingness to take Andreas for walks in the palace park — made for a much cheerier atmosphere. Two or three evenings a week, Otto Holtzman came and stayed overnight with his wife in her room downstairs. One night that week, they all visited together in Ursula's room. Otto had brought two bottles of cognac with him, some sardines, a loaf of white bread, and some jam. He brought also a gift of a wind-up toy for Andreas.

Ingeborg had never met Otto before but was not surprised

when he started right in teasing her. He was holding a canvas bag on his lap, and was rummaging through the parcels and bottles. "I had heard that Ingeborg was plain and homely," he said, to the delight of Ursula and Edda when they detected Ingeborg's reactions. She sat at the table with her hands folded just so, her face shining. She was regarding Otto indulgently, with obvious primness, her lips set. These were just the sort of blandishments that could endear a person to Ingeborg. Her jewel blue eyes went from Otto to her mother, and back again, waiting for him to produce the expected gift. At last, after much artifice, he came up with something soft wrapped in tissue.

Ingeborg flashed her mother a pleased glance before unwrapping the package before her. Her eyes widened at once. She lifted it in her hands; it was an embroidered blouse, with a pattern of delicate flowers stitched in red and blue about the yoke and cuffs. As Ingeborg was by nature all but incapable of showing excited reactions, a look of perplexity distorted her features. Her lips twisted oddly to one side, as she stared in disbelief at the wonderwork in her hands.

"That was made by my mother's sister in Prague. But I was told," Otto explained, "that I was not to give it to anyone until I had traveled far and wide to find somebody suitably pretty. You are that person," he said.

Otto was a phlegmatic, hollow-faced man with a head of grayish unkempt hair, an unruly mustache, and an apparent taste for rumpled clothing. Ingeborg had liked him on first sight. She liked the look of intense curiosity in his eyes, and the way he slouched down in his chair, his legs stretched horsily toward the porcelain stove. Otto was several years older than Edda, and Ingeborg divined at once that he probably enjoyed Edda's bossy ways. Edda had a sharp tongue. Ingeborg had been wrong in one of her guesses, however.

When she opened the wrapping paper and discovered the gift inside, she thought for a second or so that it was sent to her by Otto's employer, the lady named Berenice who had given her the patent leather shoes that she wore daily now. That was not the case. In fact, Otto and Edda knew enough about Ingeborg's father, missing on the eastern front these past months, and of the likely fate of such men, that the gifts they brought for Ingeborg and Andreas amounted to expressions of their sincerest sympathy for the children of a fallen father. Otto had said as much to Ursula on an earlier occasion. "Nothing is spared in the east. They scorched everything when they retreated in forty-one," he said of the Russians, "and coming back, they're killing and smashing everything in their path. It would be vain to think otherwise. The reports are horrendous."

If Ingeborg had heard Otto say that, it would have produced the most desperate feelings. As it was, she struggled every day to maintain her faith in the face of an omnipresent violence she did not understand. Three or four times a week now, as with the regularity of something astronomical, came the endless train of bombers overhead, lasting sometimes for hours and hours; there was a red haze almost nightly over Berlin; their house shook and jangled to the distant explosions; when the wind turned to the west, the smoke came in a pall through the streets. Sometimes, in going down to the corner pump for a pail of water, she had to hold a wet towel over her face. The smoke from Berlin was that bad. For Ingeborg, the war was something that was always there. Trains arrived at the station carrying the wounded. The hospital where her mother worked had three big horse-drawn open ambulances that were often to be seen coming or going on the Langen Bridge. Almost weekly, some classmate's dear one was reported dead. And then, too, there was always the constant strident blare of exhortative voices on the radio from the Propaganda Ministry, commanding all to struggle to their last breath to stop the barbarians.

But worst of all, most frightening of all, was the deep suspicion eating away inside her of her mother's secret despair. Ursula didn't believe anymore. That was the hardest part by far. For Ingeborg, every day was a battle. She had become a little ministry of war unto herself. She had become a country of her own. She was a country with no geography, no armed might, no allies. If in her childish heart, she comprehended that her faith made her happier than she would otherwise be, it was only human of her. In this way, without her realizing it, she had passed the point of surrender.

On this evening, though, much was made of the children's gifts. Since there was no privacy in their upstairs room, Edda Holtzman sent Ingeborg downstairs to her own place to put on her new blouse. Ingeborg came up the stairs minutes later and appeared in the doorway, displaying herself.

"It's exquisite." Ursula rhapsodized over the sight of her daughter.

"The sort of embroidery," said Edda, pointing her cigarette, "people can't do anymore."

"A lost art," Otto agreed, while reaching a glass and pouring some cognac.

Ingeborg was beaming in the limelight. She loved such attention. "*And* it's a perfect fit," she added smartly, in case they hadn't noticed.

"Indeed, it is. It's perfect, darling," said Ursula.

Ingeborg sat then at the table reading the opening pages of

the novel she had borrowed from the von Stutterheim girl, while Ursula played records, and Otto performed card tricks for Andreas. Ingeborg soon became lost in her book, although from time to time she reflected dreamily on the girl now living in the rectory across the street, and how wonderful it was, or would be, to form a friendship with such a popular and notable young lady. Up till now, Ingeborg had had difficulty making friends. Being advanced in intelligence and emotional development, she could not help being irritatingly impatient with children her own age and had always sought love and friendship with children older than herself. She rarely, if ever, succeeded, but instead found herself standing on the margin, at the edge of a cluster of bigger children, listening to them, and trying from time to time to make herself likable and interesting. At the moment, Ingeborg speculated that her beautiful blouse would be an asset, and she intended to wear it when she called on Betka von Stutterheim to return her two books. She could picture herself removing her coat in the rectory, and Betka and Frau Freytag would both marvel over her new top, over its colors and fine workmanship, especially Betka, whom Ingeborg knew to be tasteful in such matters.

Ingeborg was not paying attention to what her mother and the Holtzmans were talking about, until she heard Otto say something about Count Bertold von Salmuth-Tresckow.

Ingeborg looked up inquisitively.

"His wife will get him out," Edda was saying.

Otto objected strenuously. His face flushed suddenly. "Nobody comes out of there!" he replied.

"The count has influence."

"Influence?"

"What is the sense of being a count," said Edda, "if you don't have influence."

"You know nothing about it!" Otto's mustache actually bristled. "The so-called People's Court is not a court, Edda. Where have you been?"

Ingeborg's mother was visibly troubled by the conversation transpiring at the table. Ursula never discussed such things, but she spoke up nonetheless. "How long has he been under arrest?" she asked.

"Eight weeks. She brings him food parcels. I tell you, it's pathetic. It's hopeless. It's frightening. She'll never see him again. None of us will ever see him again."

Within a minute, Ingeborg was able to piece together what Otto was talking about. There had been news about it on the radio every day since the middle of summer. He was speaking of the special court at which hundreds of persons implicated in the July attempt to assassinate Hitler were being tried, or had already been executed. She understood further that the lady named Berenice was a countess, and that her husband was under arrest. She pretended to resume her reading, but listened in secret.

"Don't tell me," said Otto, moving his glass of cognac round and round on the table before him. "She's been in Gestapo headquarters three times. I drove her there, to Prinz Albrechtstrasse, and waited for her in the car. *I,*" he said, "am terrified just to wait. Black uniforms everywhere, guns, grim-faced guards. I don't know how she finds the courage. Don't tell me," he said, "that that's not a great woman."

"He worships her," Edda blew up a cloud of smoke.

"I do," he said, growing recriminatory in tone. "You know nothing about it. You don't know how vile it is. You can't begin to imagine. Eight high-ranking generals have been executed at the prison on Lehrterstrasse! Bismarck, our own district civil governor, the grandson of the great chancellor himself, is locked up in there."

"I am not arguing with you," Edda placated softly.

Ursula began serving the food Otto had brought, and appeared as troubled as before. Her forehead was pink at the hairline. Ingeborg knew how her mother disliked and was frightened by such talk. Ursula tried to deflect attention.

"I think we should eat now. Otto has brought such wonderful things."

Otto had the wind up. He rubbed his mustache with the back of his hand. "I couldn't do it! I couldn't go into that building. It's a charnel house!"

"Please," said Ursula, pleading now for an end to the political profanity.

"You think it isn't?" he spoke sidelong to her.

"I don't know what to think," Ursula said.

"Stop talking about them, Otto," said Edda. "We're Ursula's guests. She has a right to insist."

"I know, I know," said Otto. "But sometimes I can't help myself. I'd do anything for her. Don't you understand?" Otto's sense of social caste, which Edda sometimes resented, was apparent in his remarks. "Fourteen years ago, a week before they were married, I drove all the way from Stuttgart to Rosenheim, to her grandmother's villa there, just to deliver baskets of fruit and flowers. Can you believe that? Two hundred kilometers. She wasn't more than a schoolgirl. Now," he said, his voice grown hoarse and unreliable, "I wait for her outside the Lehrterstrasse prison." Otto, in a sudden and astonishing gesture, pulled a rosary from his coat pocket. He dangled it before them. The black beads sparkled in the electric light. Even Edda was taken aback. "This is how I wait," he said. "This is how I wait."

No one spoke after that for an interval, until Ursula closed the subject.

"It's well that you're so devoted," she said. "The world is a better place, Otto, for people like you being in it."

Moved, Otto reached up his glass. "You, also, Ursula," he said. "And you, Edda."

"I love you, Otto," said Edda.

"I know."

"I tease you," she said.

"That's all right," said Otto. "It's the cognac. It brings out the emotion." He spoke to the boy. "Andreas," he said, "play that record again for me."

Andreas was conscious that all were watching him, impressed by his ability to reset the record, the needle, and start it playing again.

Ingeborg had set her book aside and was enjoying the tasty plate of sardines and cheese, and the glass of wine her mother had poured for her; but she was thinking about a day far off in the future, when she would enter the nave of the famous church down in Munich, going in to say a prayer for her friend, whose full name she now knew was Countess Berenice von Salmuth-Tresckow. And how everyone there, in the Frauenkirche, would turn to look when she stepped very smartly up the broad center aisle toward the altar, her head in the air, and her beautiful blond hair cascading down her back, and turning to one another, say, in whispers, "That is Ingeborg Maas."

One of Ingeborg's great favorites in the days to come turned out to be Anna Freytag, Dieter's wife, the woman who took care of things in the rectory. She was always in her kitchen, and the radio was always playing. Anna was an ardent National Socialist. She listened with the most concentrated look on her face to the speeches, thrilled to the martial music, and was an active presence at the weekly political indoctrination lectures that she was expected to attend. From the first time that Frau Freytag saw Ingeborg, on the afternoon when Betka brought her home, she took to the girl. Ingeborg must have represented to her some sort of desirable human model, because Anna — who was Tyrolean by birth and upbringing, and possessed of the dark hair, squat frame, and stolidity of her Alpine farmer ancestry — called Ingeborg Maas "my little Prussian sweetheart." What was intended by this loving epithet was not altogether clear to Ingeborg, however. During all her young days, she had regularly heard such terms thrown about, as Rhinelanders, Prussians, Franconians, and such, but was not capable of perceiving what was real behind them. She guessed, though, that the thick accent in the woman's German figured somehow in the distinction.

"I didn't know that I was Prussian," Ingeborg said.

Anna bustled much about the kitchen. As a child, Anna Freytag had been afflicted with polio, and in her movements showed herself to favor her left leg. As the house was chilly and big, she wore layers of sweaters and a knitted cap. From the very start, Anna had encouraged Ingeborg to visit her at will. Ingeborg suspected Frau Freytag was lonely; and since her mother worked longer hours now, and Andreas and his little schoolmates were looked after by a collection of Hitler Youth girls at school, Ingeborg came regularly across the street. It served, too, of course, to put her in the way of Betka, with whom she was very taken.

"I wish I were a painter," Anna insisted. "I would paint you. You would wear a long dress of blue velvet — Prussian blue velvet — with ermine trim as white as snow, and little rosebuds and laurel leaves in your hair."

"I would like that," Ingeborg attested.

"I would paint you a hundred times. I would put you in a little hunting costume, with riding britches, and one of those dashing velvet hats that great people wore when riding horseback in olden times. Would you," she pursued, lovingly, "like that?"

"Yes, I would."

Anna gave Ingeborg a cup of tea and a biscuit, then launched into one of her patriotic discourses that left Ingeborg daydreaming about her father. It must have been the picture that Anna had drawn of a girl with roses in her hair, as Ingeborg recalled dimly a picture that hung in the hallway on Fasanenstrasse in Berlin. It was a portrait of a girl sitting in a bower, gazing up dreamily at a songbird. Without consciously invoking him, Ingeborg's mind had opened itself to a vision of her father. She could see him. He was standing by himself under what looked like a high porch, with his pipe in his hand; there was sunlight on the ground before him. She could not make out his face, as it was hard, except when dreaming, to call to mind someone's face. But she had a distinct sense that that was where he was right now, quiet, standing in the shadows, smoking his pipe. Here, outside the kitchen windows, it was snowing. The snow came down in a fluttery swirl. Watching it, Ingeborg tried several times to follow the descent of a single flake, but each time it was lost to the eye almost instantly in the slow, spinning general snowfall.

Anna Freytag was talking all the while.

"What worries me," she was saying, "is that you look undernourished."

Ingeborg's mind came back from its wandering to the kitchen. "I'm supposed to weigh ten pounds more than I do."

"Ten pounds!" Anna's face fell despairingly. "At your age?"

"I was measured at school."

"When were you last measured?"

"Last spring. Since then, I've grown still another inch, but I weigh the same."

"As last year?"

"Last spring."

A look of sadness clouded the woman's eyes, as she turned away. "It's not fair," she said. "The little ones should be as well off as we were as children. They shouldn't be hungry. They shouldn't be underfed."

"What are you doing?" Ingeborg asked.

Anna had opened a carton containing holiday decorations, and was pinning up silver tinfoil angels with golden wings on the wall by the pantry door. To Ingeborg, the rectory was a cold, rather empty building; but Anna was doing her best to make the kitchen homey. By now, Ingeborg didn't notice any longer how Frau Freytag limped at every step, perhaps partly because Anna was so active and lively. The Christmas season was starting, and Ingeborg concluded that Anna was just the sort of homebody that would make a wonderful fuss over it.

Ingeborg steered their conversation to the subject of Betka. In fact, every time a noise came from the direction of the front of the house, or the street, Ingeborg turned about in her chair in hopes it was Betka coming in.

"Betka grew up too fast," said Anna. "She has a very sassy tongue and does whatever it pleases her to do. She won't listen to Herr Freytag, or to me, or to anyone. Her father is an important officer in the navy, her mother is in France, at the consulate in Lyons, and we're left to guide and discipline her. She's very single-minded and stubborn."

"Do you love her?" asked Ingeborg, in a startling remark.

Anna had just stepped back to look at the flight of her tin-foil angels. "Oh," she exclaimed, "I adore the girl. How couldn't I? She's everything a girl could be. She's a treasure."

"I like her, too," said Ingeborg, murmuring it, happy at the chance to proclaim her feelings aloud.

"I wouldn't trade her for any soul on earth." Anna came impulsively then, and squeezed Ingeborg's cheeks with her thumbs. "Except for you," she whispered. "My little blue-eyed elf!"

Even while Anna was squeezing and shaking Ingeborg's cheeks, the radio in the kitchen went suddenly silent. Seconds later, a martial fanfare was broadcast, signifying an important announcement. Ingeborg noticed how profoundly Frau Freytag's behavior altered in anticipation of a pending bulletin. She was absolutely breathless; her eyes sparkled worriedly. When the music subsided, another gravid silence ensued. Then the announcer came on. In a stunning reversal of events, he reported, German armored units under the command of Field Marshal Gerd von Rundstedt had smashed through Allied forces in the West and were exploiting the breakthrough to the full. The brilliant and totally unexpected onslaught had caught the enemy utterly unawares.

Anna Freytag appeared transformed. "I knew it," she said in a thrilling voice. "It's come."

She was clasping and unclasping her hands. Going at once to the phone then, she telephoned Dieter at the military school. Yes, Dieter agreed, there was considerable excitement in the air. People were whooping in the halls, he said.

By an irony, the "little Prussian" sitting at Anna's table did not share her friend's bounding optimism. Something in Ingeborg told her that if Edda Holtzman were here, or Otto, or even Betka herself, that they would probably make a cynical face over it, or drop a wry remark. Ingeborg was too uninformed to understand the announcement, but had already begun to recapitulate inside herself the views and responses of those around her whom she adjudged wiser than others. Nor were Ingeborg's spirits much uplifted when Anna revealed a startling ignorance of geography.

"I'll bet your own father is there," she said.

"No," Ingeborg explained, "he's in Russia."

"So?" said the other. "He could be there all the same. It's not that far."

Almost unaccountably, Ingeborg's heart was plummeting. "It's very far," she said.

As matters evolved, this December day proved to be an especially dark and troublous one for Ingeborg. Arriving home, she put the radio on, as perhaps — who could tell? — there might also be a major announcement from the east? Bulletins from the Western Front were coming over the radio at regular intervals, which likened the massive German breakthrough in the forests of the Ardennes to the historic assault in May 1940 which led to the rapid fall of France. Large German tank formations, it was being said, were driving toward Amiens, designed to split the Allied armies in two. Ingeborg had earlier decided to surprise her mother today by doing some chores without having been asked. First, she had to take their ration cards and some money from the bowl in the closet to the food shop. Ursula's cards were registered at a specific store two streets distant. On returning, bearing a small quantity of sausage and fruit, and a loaf of bread from the bakery, Ingeborg set up the ironing board. Later, she wished she had not done so, however, as she was presently dealt a stunning blow.

Her mother had washed some of Andreas's and Ingeborg's shirts and blouses, along with some socks, and one of the tablecloths they regularly used. The last was a green-and-white-checkerboard cloth that was Ingeborg's favorite. Before connecting the electric iron, she closed the double layers of the draperies and switched on the lamp, which gave the room a cozy glow. She didn't want to see the snow coming down; it held bad significations for her. Ingeborg brought up half a hodful of coal from the pile in the back yard which had been allotted to this house. Then, with that done, and a small blaze going in the stove, she felt better. She unfolded the tablecloth and opened it over the ironing board. She knew herself not to be proficient yet at ironing and was very careful to sprinkle a little water as she went along, so as not to burn the linen. It was almost time for Andreas to come home, escorted upstairs by one of the Hitler Youth girls, usually either Helga Liebeck, or her sister Eleanore.

When Ingeborg had finished this task, standing up the iron, then folding carefully the green and white tablecloth, she took it to the drawer. There were other linens there, including four costly napkins that her mother prized but never used and some of her mother's own underclothes. To make room for the folded tablecloth, Ingeborg moved the pile of napkins to one side, and there, on the bottom of the drawer, revealed to her eye as something both pretty-looking and iniquitous, was a packet of five pale blue letters tied in a string! They were addressed in Ursula's hand to Sergeant Walter Maas, with his military post office number on them, but the top envelope bore blackish stampings ordering their return to the sender. Ingeborg's lips twisted to one side. She gaped in horror as she took up the parcel of letters in her hands. The date postmarked on the top envelope was in August.

Ingeborg dropped the packet in the drawer, recoiling a step or two, as from something repellent to the touch. It explained her mother's evasiveness and occasional crying fits, and why she never spoke anymore about what their life would be like when they were all together again. It explained, too, why Edda Holtzman sometimes looked at Ingeborg the way she did, with a sort of sadness and sympathy, suggesting that she and Ursula were possessed of a private and horrible knowledge that they could not share. Ingeborg felt herself deceived. Worse, she felt that her father had been deceived. Taken together, it was a vicious blow to her secret life.

When she heard Andreas on the stairs, she replaced the napkins over the packet of letters, put the tablecloth atop both, and shut the drawer.

During the evening, Ursula noticed that her daughter was not herself and queried her about it. Ingeborg was a child who was very set in her ways, who always read from one of her books in the evening after supper, and the sight of her sitting tonight on her bed, dawdling with scissors and paper, and staring into space, was unsettling.

"Have you finished your new book?" she asked.

"No."

"Is it not a good book?"

Ingeborg was sullen and slow to respond. "I like all my books."

"Otto says he has never met a young girl who could read such difficult books. He said it is very unusual."

Ingeborg continued snipping at the paper in her hands. As

she appeared to be verging on tears, not looking up, her lips compressed, her mother changed the subject.

"Would you like a bath?" she asked, her concern mounting by the minute. Ingeborg was always a pillar of even-mindedness and predictability.

"No," came the terse reply.

"Ingeborg was very fresh with Eleanore today," Andreas offered.

"Is that true?" Ursula inquired.

Ingeborg responded angrily, turning her head and gazing fixedly at an invisible spot in space. "It is not."

"She slammed the door," Andreas said.

"Did you?"

This allegation was beneath contempt, apparently, and not worthy of a response, as Ingeborg showed her brother a scathing look.

Whether this line of questioning would have brought the cause of Ingeborg's unhappiness into the open was not to be clarified tonight. Just minutes after nine o'clock, the sirens wailed. Ursula switched on the radio at once, in time to hear the announcer declaring an "Air-raid Danger 15," the most severe alert, signifying the approach of an enormous fleet of bombers. Before going downstairs, Ursula opened the windows from both top and bottom to protect against violent changes in air pressure. Searchlights were sweeping the sky in silence. Someone ran by in the street below, his footsteps ringing.

There were three camp beds in the cellar, placed along the walls parallel to the ceiling joists. The use of electric light was naturally forbidden, so they always lighted two candles. Typically, Ingeborg read while Ursula endeavored to comfort and entertain Andreas. The Falke woman, grown more eccentric, sat at a table apart from the others, toward the back of the cellar, playing solitaire by candlelight. Edda was still on her shift at the hospital and was doubtless in the downstairs shelter there by now. In about twenty minutes came the distant drone, and the flak batteries in and around Potsdam opened fire. The roar to follow, of the pounding guns and the oncoming engines, was ear-shattering in itself. Tonight, bombs were falling on Potsdam. The cellar shook with every explosion. The successive blows left Ingeborg's ears and head ringing. More than once, she saw Fräulein Falke leap to her feet and cast about in panic. From the floors above came the bang and splashing sound of windows exploding, followed instantly by the odd sucking detonation of a door blown in from its hinges. Annaliese Falke cried out in despair, and Andreas was hollering "Mommy" over and over again. A candle went out. After that, it got worse.

Everything was throbbing, as though the earth was atremble at its core. Ingeborg saw in the reduced light the silhouette of her mother sprawled atop her little brother on the camp bed across from her. Ingeborg turned to the wall and began crying. Everything was exploding. There was a vicious hissing sound in the street, of an unexploded incendiary flare rushing past on the pavement, and the simultaneous squeal of a fire truck. Somewhere, a mine went off; and in the shock of it, Ingeborg's bed hurtled sideways, scraping and bouncing across the floor. Annaliese was screaming incoherently. Running footsteps sounded in the street, accompanied by shouts. Then a lull developed. Even the flak died down.

At ten o'clock came a second and bigger wave of enemy planes. By then, and for many more minutes, the deep seismic rumblings of what was happening over Berlin were incessant. Most frightening was the report of glass exploding up and down Charlottenstrasse. The house rocked violently. The second candle was already out. Ursula called to Ingeborg in the darkness. There was no reply. As the violence diminished, though the profound droning went on and on, Ursula relighted a candle and went to inspect.

Ingeborg lay on her belly, in her purple coat, her arms extended relaxedly above her head, fast asleep.

They brought him into the cellar of the Lehrterstrasse prison at dawn. There were very bright lights on in the cellar, and two movie cameras set up on tripods left and right of the place where he was to be hanged. The noose was a piece of piano wire hanging from a meat hook. When von Salmuth-Tresckow came in, he was visibly faint; he looked bloodless and frightened. One of the cameras was already running. Now the second cameraman started his going. The executioners and cameramen stepped out their cigarettes and got to business. The man's hands were already tied behind his back. An S.S. officer ordered him to be lifted up, and the wire noose made snug around his neck. Then they let him down. He struggled. The cameras ran on. Nobody else was in the picture now, just the condemned man kicking violently in the air. His eyes were maddened; he squirmed and twisted in agony. His hair was fluffed up, and he was urinating, and kicking and swinging back and forth.

Before he was dead, an S.S. man lifted him from behind, and another man gave him a booster shot, to prolong the suffering. They set him dangling again. It took many long minutes for him to die. At the end, his feet continued to flap, as though he were waltzing. Even the cameramen laughed. The impression was comic. Finished, they shut off their equipment.

2

FOR SEVERAL DAYS THEREAFTER, Ingeborg displayed an unusual lethargy. Frau Redeker noticed it at school, as Ingeborg Maas was not only the most quick-minded student she had ever had, but one of the most alert and composed. She was the type of model student who could always be counted on to incite healthy competitive feelings in others. These days, though, were different. She was listless and inattentive. Nor did any amount of questioning by her teacher shed any light on the matter. In the end, Frau Redeker could assume only that the extraordinary pressures to which all the schoolchildren were subjected these days — the bombings, the food shortages, the ever-growing rolls of family members lost and killed — had claimed another victim. It was pitiful but common.

Each afternoon, instead of going home now, or going to visit Anna Freytag in the rectory, Ingeborg would go someplace else. It was too cold to stay outdoors. Once, she took a long walk in Sans Souci park, past the famous summer palace of Frederick the Great, circling round by the Chinese teahouse, just walking without aim or destination. She felt abandoned. Always a rather solitudinous child, Ingeborg sought comfort from her agony in her own way. Most afternoons, she went to a chapel near her school, which, although cold inside, was at least windless. It was too dark to read. The stained-glass windows were boarded up. Only splinters of light leaked through, giving the chapel a mysterious and dimensionless feel, rather holy to Ingeborg's mind. It was soothing to her undermined spirit.

There were many Russian women living in Potsdam that winter. They were laborers and household workers brought in from the east to mitigate the manpower shortage; on any day, a half dozen or more could be found forgathering in a corner of the chapel. It was their opportunity to socialize. Some brought their babies. They sat in a cluster in the near dark of the church, conversing in subdued tones. Ingeborg looked on unseeingly. Mostly, she stared into space. At some point each day, either here or somewhere, she gave in to her despair, and cried. One day, she resolved that any tears that should rise to her eyes and cloud her sight would be expended here, not at home, not at school, not in Frau Freytag's kitchen at the rectory. In fact, in her childish appreciations, she conceived the notion that a person had only so many individual tears that could be shed in any one day, or any week, a certain limited number, and that if she produced them now, in the chapel, later she would remain dry-eyed no matter what. With that rationale in place, Ingeborg put her head down on the pew in front of her, and wept copiously.

But in the dozen or so days to follow, Ingeborg recovered her strength. On one of her afternoon visits to the chapel, she overcame her most agonizing worry. It came to her inspirationally. She wished she had thought of it before. If the letters that had been sent to her father had not reached where he was, that did not mean that he was not where he was. It meant only that the letters had not got to where he was.

She saw the Russian women huddled in the church, and thought it more than likely that no one from home knew where they were; or that the whereabouts of at least one of

them was a total mystery and source of day-to-day anxiety
to somebody far away. On the day before Christmas, Ingeborg got a ten-pfennig piece from her mother for the purpose
of buying a writing tablet; but she had something else in
mind. Late that afternoon, she dropped a coin in the metal
box at the back of the chapel and took up the little stick that
people used to light candles. The word "devotion" was in
her mind. She didn't know where it came from, or where
she had learned it, unless it was in the story she read once
about a saintly lady named Xaviere, who lived in captivity
and never spoke to anyone, but knelt on "paving stones"
every morning for a year, even in rain and snow, and was
saved one day by a clever minstrel who carried her off in the
disguise of a youthful friar. For Ingeborg, the lighting of a
candle was just the sort of stately, dignified enactment that
distinguished long-suffering heroines from their quotidian
sisters. As the wick came alight inside the wine-colored
glass vessel, she continued for an interval to hold forth the
lighting stick, if only to admire the slender curve of her
wrist and the delicate lines of her fingers.

She was feeling much better. Everything was going to be
all right. Back home at dusk, she listened to Christmas
hymns on the radio, a live performance by a Lübeck choral
society; she was further cheered and uplifted when Otto and
Edda Holtzman came by and took the three of them out to
supper. This was an occasion of special delight, as Ingeborg
could barely recall from her earliest days having gone to a
restaurant with her mother and father. She knew that
lunches and dinners were still being served at places like the
Palast Hotel, and at several restaurants, despite the food
shortage, so long as the patrons brought their ration cards;
but Ingeborg had not once imagined such a rare treat for herself. Moreover, even though Otto was disallowed by state

regulations to use his automobile for personal use, he ush-
ered everyone into the car, and drove through the rubble-
strewn streets to a well-known *Weinstube* run by a man
named Felix Haberzettl, a restaurateur renowned for his re-
sourcefulness of late in continuing to provide daily fare.
Along the way, Otto pointed out the surprising number of
unregistered automobiles plying their way through the dark
streets. Many people had hidden them away against the sort
of emergency that was now at hand. What was more, Otto
pointed out, the police were ignoring them. Order was breaking down.

It was widely recognized by now, Christmas Eve, that von
Rundstedt's "great counteroffensive" in Luxembourg and
the Ardennes had stalled. Ingeborg could tell by the way
Edda alluded to it, with her smirks and innuendo, that conditions at the front lines, both west and east, were as hopeless as ever. At such times, when others could be animated
by the news, Ingeborg wondered what her mother was
thinking. Mostly, she was pleased and comforted by Ursula's philosophical calm, as it seemed to Ingeborg to be
founded on something deeper inside her, something that
Edda, for all her cynicism and knowledgeable airs, lacked.
While riding in the car, Ingeborg stole looks at her mother.
Lights of passing cars moved softly over Ursula's face. Ingeborg was touched with love feelings. She imagined that
night years ago when her mother had had to walk across the
dance floor to help her father out of his shyness, and
thought what a smart thing that was to do.

At the door of the restaurant, something of a fuss was
made over Ingeborg. That was not uncommon. She had an
inborn instinct for putting herself on display, perhaps by af-
fecting not to do so, or through the sudden flashing of an icy

smile so fleeting that it vanished the instant it appeared. In this case, though, Herr Haberzettl was well acquainted with Otto, going back to their army days in the First War, and was showing the girl a special if playful deference. After greeting Otto and the two women, Felix Haberzettl turned and bowed to Ingeborg. He actually clicked his heels.

Ingeborg loved him at once. Herr Haberzettl was a stout man, with a florid complexion, who enjoyed a reputation among his clientele as a raconteur and bon vivant. He was a flamboyant dresser, too, evident tonight in the smooth bulge of his emerald silk vest, and the little green dagger points of his pocket square. He leaned indulgently toward Ingeborg and explained in a syrupy voice why the dining room behind him was illuminated by candle only. "I must apologize," he said. "For want of our having paid our electric bill, the British turned the lights out all along the street the night before last."

Ingeborg laughed sharply and turned in delight to her mother. It was the best bomb joke she had ever heard. "It looks so pretty," she exclaimed.

"Indeed, it is that," said the man. "It makes for an intimate and romantic atmosphere. And, of course," he added, also smoothly, "your usual table is on reserve."

"Is it a big one?" Ingeborg piped gaily.

Herr Haberzettl's eyes closed and opened, and he nodded, in the way of satisfying her on that point. "There isn't a bigger one, Madame, or a better one, nor any other table positioned so close to the fire. This way, please."

Ingeborg darted sparkling looks over her shoulder at her mother as she followed the owner into the cavernous *Weinstube*. The big dining room was crowded with soldiers, she noticed; but more astonishing, an orchestra of ten musi-

cians sat on chairs on a platform at the rear and at that instant commenced playing a Schubert piece.

While walking, Herr Haberzettl leaned round to her in
confidence. "If someone is at your table, I'll have them
thrown out."

"Thank you very much," said Ingeborg, feeling quite adequate already to the owner's delightful remarks. The room
was very noisy. She admired the beamed ceiling and the
glow arising from scores of candles all about her. There were
clouds of pipe and cigarette smoke and shouts of laughter.
Ingeborg hadn't the maturity to realize that the festal holiday atmosphere derived a great deal that evening from the
growing fatalism on all sides, a general comprehension that
the war was coming to an end, and that for many the worst
was yet to come.

Once they had been seated, Ursula was touched by the
sight of Ingeborg holding the menu in her hands and study-
ing it with a prospective air. She turned to Edda. "Look at
her. She's so happy. The poor little things don't even know
what world they live in. To them, nothing is more natural
than the explosions and the sirens going off, cars burning in
the streets."

Edda was holding Andreas on her lap. "We'll all make it
through all right."

Ingeborg could not believe that the chicken dish printed
on the menu, or the mussels in wine sauce, could actually
be delivered on demand. But when Herr Haberzettl came to
the table, he was quick to reassure her on that score. He told
Ingeborg that he would personally take her order. By this
time, the collection of youthful beer-drinking soldiers at the
next table had taken an interest, smiling as Herr Haberzettl
doted on the girl.

Before sitting, Ingeborg had removed her coat; not because it was warm enough to do so, for it was not, but she wished everyone to see her in her Czech embroidered blouse. Unknown to the others, even to her mother, she had put a sweater on underneath it.

"Bring her champagne," one of the soldiers spoke up in a dry, humorous voice. "Bring her what you would never bring to the likes of us." His companions laughed over that.

"That goes without saying," said Felix, suavely. "Would mademoiselle," he inquired, "like champagne?"

"Yes, I would," said Ingeborg.

Felix noted this with pencil stub on his pad, saying, for the benefit of the others present, "No one else will be receiving champagne. You may wager your shoes on that."

"That's a beautiful little lady," said another youth.

Aware that Ingeborg had not looked up from the menu, Herr Haberzettl saw fit to respond to the soldier.

"You will notice," he said, "that she ignored you."

"They all ignore me," returned the soldier.

"She's a regular heartbreaker," suggested another, in a soft, deepish voice.

"And they will all continue to ignore me," added the first. "I am not desirable to beautiful women."

"You have Ilse," offered a third.

"That's what I mean," said the first.

Everyone appeared quite happy.

When dinner arrived, Ingeborg looked at the plate placed before her as upon an illustration in a magazine. It was beautiful to contemplate. The chicken and potato dumplings were placed just so, and there were little sprigs of some green garnish disposed about, as in a work of art. Felix presented it himself, with the air of a royal steward. He stood over her, with his cheeks flushed. A young woman wearing a heavy sweater over her aproned uniform came to the table and placed a glass of champagne next to her plate.

In case Ingeborg didn't know what it was, Herr Haberzettl helped her. He spoke deferentially into her ear. "Your champagne has arrived," he intoned.

Colored with pride, Ingeborg looked to her mother, and to Otto and Edda, as well, before reaching for the glass.

The young soldier nearby continued with his playful lament. "They don't even look at me. I'm undesirable. They sit with their back to the coal fire, sipping their champagne, and I could be a block of wood. Ilse!" he exclaimed disdainfully. "Ilse is coarse!"

Ingeborg was listening intently but could not bring herself to look at him. He was the nearest soldier to her. She felt his eyes on her.

"You," said another of the soldiers, "are coarse."

"I am coarse," he agreed.

A major sitting at the far end of the table spoke up. "Let the little girl eat her supper," he remarked casually. (Ingeborg had noticed the major when she came in; he was missing an arm; his left sleeve was pinned to his coat.)

"All of my family is coarse. My father is coarse. My mother is coarse beyond description. All my fourteen grandparents, every one of them," the soldier said.

Ingeborg laughed spontaneously at that, and stole a glance. He was watching her. He was obviously an officer-in-training, noticeably young, probably not much more than seventeen. His hair was cropped short, and he had a shiny, chiseled face. Ingeborg thought him handsome to look at. He was slouched deeply in his seat, his arm crooked over the back of his chair. Except for the major, all of the soldiers sprawled about the table were similarly youthful. Unable to hold his gaze, Ingeborg returned her attention to her chicken.

"Are you spoken for?" he asked.

Ursula and the others laughed. Ingeborg knew the meaning of the expression. "No, I am not," she replied. She reached for a dumpling with her fork, hoping to prolong the exchange, and awaited another opportunity to look at him; he had a beautiful bony face and insinuative eyes.

"You are not, then," he added, tentatively, "married."

The major, Ingeborg noticed, was laughing also now. Between bites, she replied with the sort of properness she knew they wanted her to exhibit. "I am not spoken for," she enunciated in measured tones, "and I am not married."

"You realize," the young soldier came right back, "that I am very relieved to hear that." He was showing her a very earnest look. Ingeborg liked his quickness and his wit; she liked also the way the stiff collar of his uniform set off his head; he was possessed of a very beautiful head, she thought.

"Where are you from?" Ingeborg piped, inquisitively.

"Do you know Thuringia?"

"Yes, I do."

"I'm from a village there."

"And do all of your grandparents live there? All fourteen of them?" Ingeborg made him a derisive look.

"She is too quick for you, Franzi," injected another.

"We all live in the same village," he replied, "and all have the same family name, and we are all coarse. Especially me."

Ingeborg blushed a trifle under the attention. She focused on her chicken. She asked herself if she liked the name Franzi and decided that she did. In fact, she liked it very much.

"Are you not going to look at me again?" he inquired, softly.

Ingeborg was handling her utensils just so. Ursula Maas was strict about table manners, as, Ingeborg recalled, her father had also been, and the lessons were not lost upon her. She summoned her nerve to protract the conversation.

"What is the name of your village?" she asked, in an effort at casualness.

"Hildsburghausen." He gave the name a rolling guttural inflection. "Have you ever heard of it?"

"No." She sat with her champagne glass in her fingers.

"Would you like to go there sometime?" He posed the question in the undertones of a suitor, which visibly flustered her. "We have horses and wagons. After the war, I could come for you."

"With a horse and wagon?" cried Ingeborg, with a haughtiness that brought a merry response from the young soldiers. Her next remark set off another outburst. "That *is* coarse," she said.

For a long moment, she showed Franzi a pair of scolding blue eyes.

He nodded fatalistically. "I know," he confessed. "I know."

"A horse and wagon!" she threw out with playful disdain. She was enjoying herself immensely.

She had never been flirted with before and had not known how very much fun it could be.

Otto, in the meanwhile, was apprising Ingeborg's mother of some dark facts. Ten days previous, the notorious People's Court under Judge Roland Freisler had found Count Bertold von Salmuth-Tresckow guilty of complicity in the July 20 plot to assassinate Hitler. He was executed the next morning, said Otto, in a manner too grisly to describe.

"And his wife?" said Ursula, referring to the lady in Glindowsee who had given shoes to Ingeborg.

"She is taking it well. She has been prepared for it, I think." Otto was speaking under his breath. "We found out last night."

"What about the district governor?" Edda interrupted her husband.

"He was acquitted a month ago, but they're still holding him. 'Our glorious leader' doesn't dare execute a Bismarck." Otto knocked his pipe out in an ashtray. "But for his name, Bismarck would be dead, too."

Ursula developed a knot in her stomach when people spoke as Otto Holtzman just had, as in the cynical expression "our glorious leader." Whenever possible, Ursula excepted herself from such company and pretended not to have heard. There were some things she didn't want to think about, things she couldn't afford to think about. It was enough to care for her children. It was enough to have lost Walter. She wanted only to help with the patients in her Red Cross work, and, when it was all over, to be alive enough to go on caring for her babies.

She looked across the table to Ingeborg, flirting with the young soldier, who was himself not much more than a boy. Ursula thought of the boys at the hospital, the ones who were known malingerers. They were very young and were terrified of being sent out to be killed. They lay in their beds, trying to look sick, living in dread of the doctor coming to them, today or tomorrow, and ordering them to return to their units, as he regularly, if reluctantly, would always do. And indeed, Ursula thought, many of them will be killed. She knew little about politics, geography, or war, but she knew that her country was ringed in fire.

Staring at Ingeborg, her heart filled with feelings of both

love and admiration for her firstborn. Ingeborg was truly, as Ursula often said, her strength. The sight of her daughter, with a champagne glass in her fingers, her long tail of blond hair spilling down her back, cast Ursula into a reverie.

When Ingeborg remarked on Franzi's coarseness, and everyone laughed, Ursula turned and smiled at the major. He bowed his head in response.

Otto asked Ursula about the American bomber that had come down in the trees at the golf club outside Potsdam two afternoons ago.

"We sent out a rescue team," said Ursula. "They found three alive and brought them in."

Andreas was trying to get his mother's attention. "What do they look like?" he said.

"Like anyone else," said his mother.

That reply perplexed Andreas, as he thought the men going over in the planes would look very different.

"What do they say?" asked the boy.

"We are not allowed to speak to them."

"How many enemy fliers are there at the hospital?" Otto was curious to know.

"About twelve," said Edda.

"Yes, twelve," Ursula confirmed. "All Americans. Mostly they're badly burned, covered in bandages. One of them is up and about and allowed to do chores. In fact, he went out with the rescue team. Besides the three they brought in by ambulance, a fourth was found dead in a tree."

When it came time for the tableful of young soldiers to break up and depart for the evening, the major with the missing arm came over to Ursula's table and introduced himself to her. He was visibly old school. He had a dueling scar and exhibited a stiff correctness that might have masked the attraction he felt for Ursula. He had been stealing looks at her for nearly an hour. "I hope my pupils," he said, "have not offended you or your daughter with their teasing."

Ursula was smiling up at him. "I think my daughter was very charmed," she said. "I'm sorry that your boys aren't home for Christmas. And you, as well," she added.

He signified the youths with his eyes. "This has become my Christmas. This is as much a father as I'll ever be again."

Ursula understood instantly what he was saying. "I'm sorry to hear that," she said softly.

Otto and Edda looked on with interested, respectful expressions during the exchange.

Ursula reached up her hand. "I am Ursula Maas."

The major gave his name as Paul Frings and inquired if she lived in Potsdam.

"Yes, I do," Ursula responded politely. "On Charlottenstrasse. I work as an aide at one of the hospitals."

The major was unexpectedly frank. "Your husband is with the military?" he said.

Ursula's face changed. She looked about to be certain her children were not listening. "He is officially listed as 'missing, presumed dead.' "

"You have my heartfelt condolences," said the major.

"He was a signalman with the 168th Infantry in the Baltics," she added, forlornly.

"I am very sorry."

Otto and Edda pretended now not to be listening. Edda had taken Andreas onto her lap, as he appeared sleepy, and was whispering into his hair. Otto was staring at his hands. Across the table, the young soldier was bidding Ingeborg a good night. He was standing by her chair, gathering up his gloves, coat, and hat. "I will come for you one day —"

"With your wagon?" she exclaimed. Ingeborg was by now

at her charming best, showing the shiny-faced youth a look
of teasing disbelief.

"Naturally, the wagon will be decorated," he assured her.
"It will not be an ordinary farm wagon. There'll be no tools,
or livestock feed, or anything like that."

"*Livestock feed?*" Ingeborg was in her element, especially
as all on hand, including the major, were attentive to her
showmanship.

"I think that the champagne has produced an effect on my
daughter," said Ursula to the major.

He smiled at the idea. "It's not impossible," he agreed.

"Mind you," Franzi cautioned Ingeborg against unwar-
ranted expectations, "it will not be a carriage."

"It doesn't sound like it!" she piped right back. She was
turning this way and that in her seat, casting quick glances
at her mother, then at the others.

"It will not have carriage wheels, nor," said Franzi, "will
it have wagon wheels. I can't come all the way on the autobahn from Hildsburghausen on steel wheels."

"Will it have any wheels?" She pinched her lips reproach-
fully.

"It will have automobile wheels."

Ingeborg clapped a hand to her head. "*Rubber tires?*" she
cried. "A farm wagon with rubber tires?"

With his coat buttoned, Franzi straightened to full height
as though hurt and offended by the young lady's ridicule.
"It's three hundred kilometers from Hildsburghausen."

"I would never ride in a farm wagon, certainly not with
fat rubber tires. Pulled by a horse? On the autobahn?"

Franzi's companions were gathered round, putting on
scarves and overcoats. "Merry Christmas, Ingeborg," said one
of them. "I think you are going to make Ilse very jealous."

"Ilse!" said Franzi, turning to the other. "Ilse has become for me like a little barn owl."

Ingeborg loosed a high, piping laugh.

"My mind is all filled up now — with somebody new," he said, in soft nostalgic tones. He brushed the top of his cap with the sleeve of his coat. "Someone new has stolen her way into my heart."

Ingeborg was unable to stop laughing.

"I believe you are right about the champagne," said the major, as he prepared to take his leave.

"Good night, Ingeborg," said another soldier.

"I think I shall never be the same," Franzi continued his romantic lament. He struck a dreamy air. "I think I shall never be the same old Franzi, known to his bosom friends in the Wehrmacht as having once been a carefree and happy-hearted fellow." With that, and with a look of sadness in his face, he turned on his heel and marched away into the crowded room.

Ingeborg sat at her place, giggling uncontrollably.

She would like to have told Betka about Franzi, the officer-in-training, and how charming and beautiful he was, and how he had flirted with her during that entire wonderful holiday supper at Herr Haberzettl's, but she knew that the older girl, at fourteen, would make small of it. Ingeborg spent two afternoons that week in the rectory across the street. Despite their difference in age, Beatrice von Stutterheim enjoyed Ingeborg's company, especially as Ingeborg showed an appreciation of her makeup and her skills in the use of it.

"Where do you get such wonderful things?" Ingeborg marveled over the older girl's fashion articles.

"My sister sends them from Budapest."

"They have these things in Budapest?"

They were visiting in Betka's room on the second floor, sitting side by side on a bench in front of an old vanity with a clouded mirror. The room was icy; the girls wore their sweaters and coats. Betka was showing Ingeborg how she applied shadow to her eyes, employing a little brush. Ingeborg had once seen some foreign fashion magazines, with ads depicting beautifully made-up ladies, and had thrilled to them. She thrilled, also, to Betka's proud and independent nature, to her cocky rebelliousness, and looked on enraptured as the older girl carefully beautified her face. She liked looking at Betka's face. Betka had become very important to Ingeborg. Until now, Ingeborg had never known anyone whom she could proudly call her friend. To think that her first true friend should be someone as illustrious as the von Stutterheim girl, whom everyone envied and emulated, especially when every day found their living conditions growing harsher, was such good fortune.

Ingeborg would liked to have made up her own face, but Betka had already ruled out that possibility. "Makeup is for women," she said, and watched in the mirror for the ten-year-old's reply.

"I know that," Ingeborg murmured.

The wintry light spilling in through the windows cast a dreary spell over the room. The armoire and vanity looked cheap, almost ramshackle. The linoleum floor covering was worn black in places. Ingeborg guessed that the previous occupants of the rectory, the pastor and his wife, had been poor. Now and then, cold whistling sounds came from the windows.

"After the war," Ingeborg asked, "will there be lots of beautiful magazines and clothes to buy?"

"Yes, there will."

In a moment of ardor, Ingeborg blurted, "I like looking at your face, Betka."

"There!" said the other, setting down her lipstick tube and turning her face to Ingeborg. Her eyes sparkled and her cheekbones were prettily highlighted. "Is that good?"

"It's beautiful!" Ingeborg's passion informed her words.

Betka was just the sort of heroine that Ingeborg favored above all. There were different types. There were delicate maidens with gentle ways who were sweet and trustful in disposition and who sometimes had to be rescued from evil circumstances. Betka was not like that. She could picture Betka von Stutterheim wearing a shiny armor breastplate and emerging on horseback from beneath the portcullis of an ancient fortress, with a dozen loyal archers following hurriedly on foot behind her. Betka had a heroic dimension. Ingeborg liked the girl's vigor, the way she walked, her profile, the dark wave of her hair. Presently, she betrayed her childish nature with an ingenuous question. "May I tell people that we're friends?" she said.

"We are friends," said the other, briskly. "That's why you're in my room."

"Thank you," said Ingeborg.

They sat side by side on the bench for a half hour or more, the gray daylight leaking out of the room. Ingeborg was wearing a pair of blue woolen gloves that Edda had lent her; they matched her coat and scarf, even if her coat was getting noticeably short in the sleeves. When she was sitting with her arms on her lap, she could retract her wrists in such a way that no one noticed the shortness of the plum-blue coat.

"Saturday," Betka promised, "I'll take you to the movies at that place on Franzosischestrasse, the theater by the church." Betka was putting away her things. She kept her makeup articles in an old apricot suede pouch with a zipper.

By the time Ingeborg departed for home, despite the bleak light of dusk that made stencils of the trees, and the sound of a loose-hinged door banging somewhere in the wind, she carried Betka's image before her mind. Tonight, she would plan what things to say to Betka when they went to the movies Saturday. She suspected that Betka von Stutterheim was the only person there was from whom she would not keep a secret. She wished she had a secret to share. She imagined sitting on the vanity bench in front of the dully lighted mirror, with Betka before her, and admitting to some important fact or intelligence about herself, and how the von Stutterheim girl would be moved by that, and put her arms around her.

In the hour before Ursula and Andreas returned home, Ingeborg made up her mind to send her father something in the mail. She had never done that before. She copied the address from one of the envelopes hidden in the drawer, found a stamp for it, and sealed it. On the back, she wrote the return address. The letter in its brevity was both childish and exact. It said, "I know you are safe. I am waiting for you."

Darkness was falling when she went out to the corner mailbox and posted it.

Until now, the hardships to be borne had been difficult. The raids were naturally the worst of it, the days and nights spent hiding in shelters, the sudden paralyzing fear whenever bombs came crashing down nearby. There was the thick yellow smoke that came drifting back from Berlin, and clung for hours sometimes over Potsdam. People going through the streets clutched wet towels to their faces. But the town was by no means devastated. There were fallen buildings on every street, but the famous old garrison town, with its profoundly beautiful architecture, was largely intact. During the previous summer, there were still swans floating serenely on the Havel, past the stone steps adjacent to the town castle. Ingeborg — in her secret heart, although she never revealed it in words — would have been happy to continue living in Potsdam, had her father wished them to do so. She loved the way you could see the dome of St. Nicholas from just about anywhere. She was particularly taken, too, with the look of the town castle colonnade, and the way someone, years ago, had planted linden trees next to it (in what appeared to be big flowerpots). She liked the Old Market, with its venerable town hall, and the way the trams all crisscrossed there. Even Charlottenstrasse, she felt, was quite grand, as was the park, called the Wilhelm Platz, not more than two streets away.

But day by day now, the mood grew noticeably darker. People snapped at each other; everyone was short-tempered. For Ingeborg, the most appalling episode so far took place during this same January week, while she was at school. It began with the sirens wailing and all the children being shepherded hurriedly into the basement. For a long time now, the raids coming in toward Berlin were enormous, with the sky sometimes glittering with planes from one end to the other. The roar was like that of a dozen railroad cars rolling through the rooms overhead. The foundation of the school shook relentlessly. Some of the children became hysterical. Others laughed wildly and wet their underclothes.

This morning, two of the older boys went outdoors with Axel Sprague, the school custodian, and started up the auxiliary generator, piping air into the cellar. On this day, Potsdam was being hit. Ingeborg was one of three or four children in her group who was not crying. She sat in terror, with her legs drawn up, her head buried in her knees, her hands over her ears. It was just when the sound of the thunderous flak and the unearthly pounding of the engines overhead was subsiding that the school annex, the two-story brick building adjoining their own, received a direct hit. The bomb penetrated the roof and both floors, and exploded in the cellar across the way. Ingeborg was thrown ten feet under the impact, scraping headfirst across the cement floor. Dark blood bubbled from the heels of her hands. The detonation had blown in the windows. Window boarding, canvas, and exploded glass lay everywhere. The air smelled gassy, and the temperature was going up. Frau Redeker was on her feet, shouting, "No one's in the annex! No one's in the annex!" She was visibly deranged. In fact, the cellar of the school annex was too shallow to be used during raids. That was what Frau Redeker had meant. Ingeborg was on her knees, staring in shock at her bleeding hands. Many children were calling for their mothers. That was when it happened.

From across the play yard came a secondary explosion. The annex erupted in flames. The sun was shining, and the sudden bright jets of flame bursting simultaneously from all the windows seemed momentarily a facet of the morning sun. Ingeborg was one of a half dozen children who saw what followed. A door flew open, and the elderly Herr

Geissler came hurrying out into the schoolyard. In his long black coat and copious mop of white hair, he was on fire from head to foot. His hair was burning like a candle. Ingeborg screamed. The look of pain in Herr Geissler's face was like something borne in from another world. He ran a half dozen frantic, tottering footsteps into the yard, and then simply dismantled in the air, and went down. Boys going outdoors could not get close to him for the heat. He was fuel-soaked. The flames rolling over him made a pale glow in the sunlight. For near to an hour, before an emergency team arrived from the nearest fire brigade, he lay in the play yard, a smoking, incandescent heap.

Ingeborg was not the same for days to come. She had endured many frights in the past two years, but it was the immolation of the venerable professor, with his eyes straining skyward and his long black-coated figure disintegrating in flight right before her eyes, which left her stupefied. She stayed home for three days with a severe cold, immersing herself as best she could in her romances. She ate the meals her mother was able to prepare without appetite. It was more than a week before she stopped in at the chapel again, or visited Betka, or Anna Freytag, in the rectory across the way.

Betka von Stutterheim was her usual resilient self these days, but the older woman, Ingeborg saw, had grown uncharacteristically quiet and disconsolate. Even the most indomitable believer in the Hitler order and in the invincibility of German arms saw the writing on the wall, with the most dreaded of all possibilities coming to pass. By the end of January, enemy forces were approaching the Rhine on a broad front. Even scarier were developments in the East. Warsaw had fallen on the eighteenth of the month, and Soviet troops had broken into East Prussia. Looting and raping were epidemic. Nearly all radio reports from Berlin had taken on a desperate, fanatical character. Even the local party leaders, in their weekly indoctrination lectures, called for fighting to the last man. Fifteen-year-old boys were being assigned to the local flak batteries. Trains crowded with the wounded arrived daily.

For the first time, panic was becoming a palpable presence. Ingeborg was relatively fortunate, as her mother gave off a reassuring calmness. Her work at the hospital was so governed by an air of emergency and the need to grapple with minute-to-minute crises of life and death, that it fortified her against larger, more abstract fears. One day, when Ursula was confessing her ignorance of politics and world events to Edda Holtzman, Ingeborg heard Edda characterize her mother as "the salt of the earth." Ingeborg fancied that expression, and it came to mind on many occasions. Somehow, she knew what it meant. When her mother came in the door, after long hours at the hospital, carrying a parcel of eggs and bread from the food shop, and smiling cheerily at her and Andreas, that was what it meant. And day by day, helped by that, Ingeborg got stronger inside and more clearheaded about everything. When Andreas came down with the flu in early February, Ingeborg was prepared to do what was necesssary to make him well.

Ursula explained to her daughter certain perils.

"If we are undernourished," she said, "and we get sick with the flu, or scarlet fever, it is dangerous to the heart. He has to be kept warm and well fed."

"I'm not hungry, Mommy," said Ingeborg.

"That's not what I meant. You need your nourishment, too. Edda and I will try to get extra things for him to eat from the canteen at the hospital."

"I'll read to him, if he would like," Ingeborg offered. She

felt vaguely guilty about something that she could not iden-
tify.

"That would be nice," said Ursula. "You don't pay too
much attention to him, you know."

Ingeborg felt a sudden stab of remorse. Her mother had
never said that before. They were standing on the stair head
outside their door, discussing her brother in soft tones. Ingeborg felt the tears coming. "I am too selfish."

"You are not selfish. You are egotistical, and that's not a
bad thing to be. It's going to make me very proud of you
when you're grown up," she said, "maybe even prouder of
you than I am now."

"I hope so," Ingeborg muttered.

What Ursula said next affected the girl deeply.

"We wouldn't want to lose Andreas, would we?"

Ingeborg set her fist to her forehead and remained speechless. That was one prospect that had never, never entered
her mind. There were many horrible things that could happen at any moment, but that bleak possibility — of losing
Andreas — had never seemed one of them. Andreas's future
had seemed until now as assured as the moon in the sky.
"No," said Ingeborg.

For several days running, Ingeborg played the part of the
little mother. She begged a fruit tart from Annaliese downstairs and a boiled egg from Anna Freytag. She moved Andreas's bed close to the stove; she arranged his blankets and
plumped his pillows. She read him one of Karl May's most
popular Wild West stories, this with a distinctly formal and
pedagogical manner and voice, while seated beside him on a
hard chair. The boy listened in raptures. He had never heard
Karl May before. The treatment overall was, in point of fact,
salubrious. Until now, Andreas Maas had looked upon his
big sister as an authoritarian figure whose quick tongue and

flashing eyes were like admonitions signaled from a mountaintop. But now, even when down in the cellar during raid warnings, Ingeborg was a model of sisterly devotion.

For his part, Andreas had no cause to complain, nor did he show a sign of unhappiness. He stayed in bed and soaked up the attention for all it was worth. Sometimes, as though to test Ingeborg, Andreas made so bold as to ask her for something — such as a pad and pencil, or a biscuit — only to look on then in disbelief as Ingeborg got to her feet with a sweet if glacial smile, fetched what he wanted, and came back to him with some appropriately buttery phrase. In truth, she had probably never been so condescending toward anyone in her life. But to Andreas, her spoiling of him was a powerful tonic. In practically no time, he was up and about, thoroughly restored.

From those days and weeks onward, though, the general conditions of everyday life for Ingeborg and her family deteriorated steadily. One day when going downstairs to the back yard to bring up some coal from the nearly depleted winter allotment, Ingeborg found that what was left was burning. It had been on fire since the raid of the night before. Two water pipes were now broken down permanently, which required her to fetch water by the pailful everyday from the corner pump. Matters were further exacerbated, and on a large scale, by civilian refugees arriving in ever-growing numbers, pushing west to avoid the developing Soviet onslaught. As nonmilitary personnel could not obtain passage by railroad, they came in mostly on foot — women, children, and the elderly, toting whatever belongings they could carry. By the end of February, the local Potsdam police were powerless to stem the tide. Requests for a show of identification papers were met with sullenness, a cynical re-

fusal to comply, even menacing looks or threats. No less unsettling were the armored movements in the opposite direction. Twice, at dawn, long columns of German tanks rum-
bled directly through the streets of Potsdam, coming from
the nearby training center at Krampnitz, and rolling east toward Berlin.

While Ingeborg was naturally bewildered by the unpre-
dictability of things and the gathering confusion, her young
life had been such that she was resigned to ever greater hardship. That was her understanding of things, that tomorrow
would be harder than today because all of the days she had
lived through so far had been harder than their yesterdays.
Only once, though, during this period, had she given expression to her deepest impulses, to the natural rosy expectations of youth. It was one of the evenings following the
death of Herr Geissler in the schoolyard, when she went unexpectedly to her mother, without forethought of any sort,
and threw herself on her mother's lap. She was sobbing. "I
want to go back to our house in Berlin. I want Papa to be
there. I want to go back to my old school. I want Frau Stahl
as my teacher again . . . I want to go home!"

Ingeborg later upbraided herself for having surrendered to
weakness that night. She felt certain by now that no one's
faith, not even her mother's, was equal to her own — just as
she knew for certain that the street she lived on in Berlin
had been reduced to wreckage and rubble and that she could
never return to that life. To compensate, she let herself
dream about a day to come, after her father's return, when
the four of them would occupy a new house. It would be
in some village, a place unlike Berlin or Potsdam, where
bombs had never fallen, or ever would fall. She pictured a
gingerbread house in a forest town, or maybe a house in a

fishing village whose windows looked out on a harbor with boats in it. Sometimes, in her daydreams, she saw Franzi, the young soldier with the beautiful cheekbones and the flirtatious manner, coming to call on her. This last figure came to mind one afternoon when Ingeborg was bathing herself. She had warmed a pot of water on the electric heater and was sponging her body. The air outdoors was often so smoky that everyone was always quite dirty. As there was no coal any longer, she stood directly in front of the heater, scrubbing herself. She had heard Edda remark to her mother how "thin" she was; she could see the truth in it herself, in the mirror, in her birdlike limbs, hipbones, and ribs.

Ingeborg took hold of her hair in both hands and let it spill down over her breastless chest. It fell almost to her waist. She liked the effect it produced in the mirror and wondered what it would be like one day to have breasts. She could imagine it. She could imagine her breasts hidden behind the white-blond hair. She could almost feel them. Pivoting, she regarded herself from different angles. She pouted; she smiled modestly; she affected a look of alluring candor. That last one was her favorite. She rehearsed it. Shivering, she put her mother's dark green robe over her shoulders, re-arranged her hair as before to cover her chest and belly, and prepared again that candid, seductive look. She fortified the look with certain thoughts. She imagined Franzi looking through the glass at her, waiting for her to speak. He had asked her a question. She turned this way and that on her heel. She adjusted the angle and lift of her chin. She showed him then that alluring supercilious expression. Her eyes sparkled.

Turning once more, she closed the robe before her, let her hair spill down as before over both shoulders covering her front, then pushed the robe up in such a way as to reveal in its folds behind her cascading hair the outline of her future breasts. The effect was impressive to the eye. In the dusky room, her hair fell in a pale silken veil over the imagined swelling of her chest. Ingeborg was thrilled by the illusion. The glow of the electric heater illuminated her face wonderfully, while casting shadows under the contour of her bosom. That her mother's voluminous robe concealed Ingeborg's undernourished condition naturally heightened the overall effect.

It was pleasant to contemplate, as Ingeborg sometimes did, a day in future times when the young Franzi would come to visit her in her father's house. Her father would call upstairs to her. She would be sitting like Betka at a vanity, preparing her makeup. She would not hurry. He would have to wait long minutes for her. With such thoughts in her mind, Ingeborg gazed dreamily at the full-length image of herself in the mirror.

That evening, arriving home early from the hospital, Ursula was visibly worried. She had been able to get nothing at her food shop. Edda, who was off duty that day, came upstairs with Andreas, whom she had been watching. Ingeborg was troubled, as she had been waiting for supper, and was, as always, hungry. Edda asked about Ursula's ration cards.

"I have enough cards," she said. "There was no food. There was nothing."

"The shop was open?" Edda asked in perplexity.

"He kept it open from politeness," said Ursula. "Just to explain to his customers that he had exhausted what provisions he had. He said to try tomorrow." Ursula looked anxiously at Ingeborg and Andreas, who sat waiting to eat. Edda went downstairs to telephone Otto. Ursula asked

Ingeborg if she thought that Anna Freytag, the housekeeper in the rectory nearby, might be able to help. Ingeborg was not reluctant to ask and said she would try. She put on her coat and hurried downstairs. The street was dark and uncustomarily deserted, except for a man putting up garish posters exhorting all citizens to struggle to the last. It was very cold tonight. The twigs of the trees made icy clicking sounds. There was snow in the bottom of a bomb crater and a gleaming furrow of snow along the foundation of the rectory.

On this evening, Anna's husband, Dieter, was at home. When Ingeborg explained her plight, and what her mother needed, Dieter spoke up unpleasantly. He was sitting by the stove, fully dressed, in a sweater and suit and tie. Frau Freytag, who loved Ingeborg, ignored her husband's grumbling complaint and gave the girl a pot of cabbage soup to be heated up at home. Ingeborg carried the pot outdoors with great care, watching her step on the cobbled street, anxious lest she drop it. Far off, the dome of St. Nicholas etched itself on the night-lit sky, while the silhouette of a shattered building on the next street, with gaping windows, imparted a desolate feeling. The man with the posters was gone.

Edda had not been able to reach Otto by phone, but the woman downstairs, Annaliese Falke, had given her a half loaf of white bread. Edda sliced the bread while Ursula warmed the soup on the electric heater. Ursula made a point of setting their places just so, as if to compensate for the watery soup and bread. After supper, when Andreas complained of being hungry, Edda got some jam from her room downstairs and spread it on the last slice of bread for the two children. Ingeborg refused her portion. She saw herself as above such special indulgence. She washed and dried Frau

Freytag's pot. Andreas sat on the bed, eating the bread and jam while turning the pages of a picture book.

Twice during the evening, after the children had fallen asleep, there arose from the street below the sound of a column of refugees, an eerie shuffling punctuated by the cold ringing of wheels and horses' hooves on the paving stones. To Ursula, peering from the draperies, it was an ominous and dismaying spectacle, the dark, bundled figures, the mechanical pace, the horses steaming. Some of the wagons and carts laden with belongings were pulled by hand.

Edda remarked on it later. "Otto says this is just the beginning. It's all gone, Utsie."

"Is it true about Dresden?" Ursula asked.

"It's a smoking heap. Upper Silesia is gone. People are fleeing all along the Oder. Otto says that in two weeks the entire German population will be walking west on every road and highway there is — and we'll be among them."

"Please," Ursula protested.

"You hear it at the hospital, don't you?"

"Five young men were decorated for bravery this afternoon in their beds. I can't tell you how many convalescents have got up and gone voluntarily back to the front. They're sick, Edda. Their hands shake as they pull on their clothing. I'm very proud of them."

"It's their duty," said Edda.

"I have the same duty. The hospital over at Hermannswerder is so crowded that most of them are kept outdoors in tents."

In fact, in the days to come, many of the wounded were evacuated by truck and ambulance from all four local hospitals. By then, too, the food shortage was growing critical. One evening, there was nothing to eat for Ursula and the children but bread soaked in chicken fat. Some of Ursula's ration cards had expired without her having been able to make use of them. The worry showed on her face. For Ingeborg, however, something transpired during that week in March that was more dispiriting and troubling to her than the pangs of hunger that knotted her stomach. It was the discovery that Betka von Stutterheim was moving out of Potsdam. It struck Ingeborg a hard blow.

She had gone across to the rectory, ostensibly to return a book, but eager as always to visit and to be flattered and spoiled a bit by her friend. She worshipped the older girl. Betka was everything that Ingeborg prized in a young woman and that she herself hoped to be in future days. Entering the house, she found Anna Freytag packing up her kitchen things. Betka, she said, was in her room. Upstairs, Ingeborg found the von Stutterheim girl putting her things into three open suitcases.

Ingeborg was standing in the doorway with a sinking heart. Until this moment, she had not known how much her own steadiness and strength were a distillation of the great happiness at having been befriended by such an important and admired young woman. For weeks, she had thrilled to the older girl's acceptance of her as an esteemed companion.

"Where are you moving to?" she asked, quite confused.

"To my grandfather and grandmother. They live near Ulm."

Ingeborg remained in the doorway. She felt shattered. She was holding the borrowed book in her hands. She wore a big pair of her mother's mittens and a long black scarf; her coat was buttoned to her throat. She struggled to hold in her tears. *"But why?"* she said.

Betka straightened up and pointed a long arm, in impersonation of her father's authoritarian manner. " 'Go to Ulm.' My father doesn't give reasons."

Ingeborg did not laugh, however, but stared in stupefaction at her dark-haired friend.

"You may keep all these books." Betka waved at her bookcase.

"You're leaving your books behind?" Ingeborg was reduced to simple instinctive utterances. Day by day, everything was being taken from her.

"I have hundreds and hundreds of books at home," said the other. "My parents have a library. Besides, I can only take three bags."

"Is Frau Freytag leaving also? And Herr Freytag?"

The other nodded. "A car is coming in a few minutes."

Until this day, Ingeborg had spoken only once or twice to Betka about her own father, other than to say that he was on the Russian front. She had not told Betka anything, either, about the beautiful soldier named Franzi, whom she often thought about. Now, while watching Betka close up a suitcase, in a moment of weakness, Ingeborg let fall one of the few lies she had ever told.

"When my father comes home," she said, "we're going to move away from Potsdam also. . . . He is going to take us to a place called Hildsburghausen."

Betka closed the metal snaps of the suitcase. "Where is that?"

"It's three hundred kilometers from here," she replied, "in Thuringia. I have never been there. It's very pretty. . . . It's a village," she added, pathetically.

Betka sensed the passion in Ingeborg's voice and turned to her. "I'll write to you from Ulm, Ingeborg."

Ingeborg strove to conceal her feelings. Somehow, she had no faith in ever again seeing or hearing from her friend. She said nothing in response. Then, after a moment had elapsed, she took the book she was holding in her hands, stepped forward into the room, and placed it carefully on Betka's vanity.

Betka tried again. "We will write back and forth. When the war is over, you'll come visit me."

Ingeborg made no reply to that either. She looked out the window to where she could see through the trolley wires to a portion of the gray stucco facade of her own house. Oddly, from somewhere across the way came the sound of a piano. Someone was playing the piano beautifully. When Betka came to where Ingeborg Maas was standing, and put her arms around her, Ingeborg shut her eyes tightly. A few minutes later, when she left the rectory, she was carrying Betka's suede makeup kit. It was Betka's farewell gift to her. Under other circumstances, she would have been thrilled to come into possession of such an exciting collection of things, if only to play with them in private, with the little brushes and tubes and soft colors.

When she came out to the street at twilight, there was a battered field gray army car parked by the tree in front of the rectory. A soldier sat at the wheel, smoking. Ingeborg carried the little makeup pouch in both hands. The soldier nodded as she went by. He was evidently waiting for Betka and the Freytags.

Otto Holtzman came by that night, bringing two bottles of brandy and some canned corned beef, for which Ingeborg's mother thanked him profusely. It was on this night that Otto paid Ursula a memorable and heartfelt tribute, a compliment that impressed Ingeborg immensely. He said, "You're more than just the best mother there is. You're like the mother-principle itself, I swear. You're what life is all about. Edda and I have said it a hundred times."

Ingeborg watched a flush of embarrassment color her mother's face.

Edda chipped in her own view. "You're the only person I have ever met in whom there is nothing wrong."

Ursula ran a finger along her hairline, and reached for one of Edda's cigarettes. "I," she stated, "think you exaggerate, to put it mildly."

"I think not," said Otto.

Later, when the subject of the von Stutterheim girl came up, Otto Holtzman said that her father was a very highly placed Nazi official whose affiliation with the party went back to its beginnings in the Munich beer halls.

"Otto knows everybody," said Edda, airily.

Otto opened a bottle. "Most of the blue bloods have been cashiered by now. Hitler detests them."

"He's had good reason to do so since last summer," Edda remarked snidely on the July 20 assassination attempt by von Stauffenberg and others to kill the dictator.

"Bunch of amateurs," said Otto, speaking into his glass of brandy, as he lifted it to his lips.

Ursula had already prepared fried potatoes and was delighted with Otto's corned beef. Ingeborg sat at the table, listening to the adults. She didn't want to read tonight. She couldn't concentrate. Tonight, more than usual, the eyes in the framed photograph of her father seemed to be looking at her. That, she knew, was because of Betka. He wanted her to know that all her disappointments and all the sadnesses would culminate one day in one ringing triumph. He was coming toward her. In some faraway place, in Russia, or Poland, or up in the bleak, windblown farm country of East

Prussia which she had once read about in school, he was coming along a roadside under poplar trees. He had many miles to go. His boots were dusty; he looked unwell. He was walking home.

After supper, a knock came at the door. It was Herr Welt, the party block warden. He was the man who lived across the yard below the side window, and who kept a garden in the summer. He was their neighbor.

Edda Holtzman, visibly influenced by the brandy she had drunk, commenced making tart remarks the instant the man identified himself.

"What do you want?" she snapped at him.

Ursula sought at once to mollify the block warden. "Pay her no mind," she said gently.

"I am trying to keep track of more than five hundred people," Herr Welt protested. "Your house has been added to my district."

"Then why don't you talk to the house?" said Edda.

He was a stocky man who wore big spectacles, and blinked rapidly whenever he was confused or frustrated. Looking into the room, he recognized the girl with the long tail of blond hair who was sitting at the table. It was the girl he had often seen sitting in her upstairs window, reading. Herr Welt smiled weakly, and actually bowed his head a trifle in her direction.

In the very next second, Edda lashed out at him. "Where are the Führer's secret weapons?" she said.

The instant Ursula heard that, her face reddened, and she politely forced Herr Welt to step back into the hallway, where she endeavored to make small of her friend's inebriation.

"I am compelled to report this," said Herr Welt.

Otto had meanwhile laid a restraining hand over his wife's wrist, but Edda was possessed of a rancorous nature. "Report me to whom?" she threw out in a big voice. "Generalissimo Stalin?"

"I am going to report and denounce that woman!" cried the other, peering over Ursula's shoulder.

"What happened to our parades? Where are our marching bands?" Edda called out, drunkenly.

Positive that her mother was right, and that Edda was doing something stupid and perilous, Ingeborg got up and went to the hallway. She had noticed the way their neighbor had greeted her, and knew that if she put herself at her mother's side, that the man from the house next door would likely do nothing to harm them. She even had the presence of mind to close the door behind herself. Like most people these days, Herr Werner Welt was showing signs of the growing tension. He stood back a step or two with widened eyes and flushed cheeks; he was jittery and quick-tempered; he blinked constantly. He was noticeably upset by Edda's toxic remarks.

"Defeatism is dealt with most harshly," he asserted.

"Please make an allowance," Ursula attempted to minimize the matter. "We work long hours together at the hospital. She's overworked. She's hysterical."

"I do my best," said Herr Welt. "To say such things — in these desperate hours, when everyone is trying so hard — is unforgivable."

While they spoke, Ingeborg looked back and forth from her mother to the block warden. Indeed, Herr Welt looked quite harassed. He readjusted his thick-rimmed spectacles with his stubby fingers. He was wearing a swastika armband on the sleeve of his black winter coat and some type of visored cap that looked like that of a railway porter.

"I agree," Ursula placated.

"Yesterday," he continued, "two deserters were found hiding among the bomb ruins out at the Babelsberg movie studios. They were both shot." Feeling that he had spoken out of turn in the presence of the young girl, the block warden coughed into his fist. "We are all living in hardship, Frau Maas. I," he said, "have scarcely eaten in days." He looked at Ingeborg.

She was standing a foot behind her mother with her back to the door. She was staring at him. She felt almost certain that Herr Welt, when he paused to cough, had stolen a downward look at her ankles and legs.

"I'm going to give you a little brandy to take home with you," said Ursula, in a quiet, intimate tone. Herr Welt raised a hand of protest, but Ursula went into their room and closed the door behind her.

The stoutish man smiled nervously at Ingeborg, and, as before, bowed his head slightly in salutation. Ingeborg had already made up her mind to present the minor party official with one of the looks she had cultivated in the mirror. She was standing perfectly straight, with her shoulders back, her lips compressed. When Herr Welt returned his gaze to her a moment later, he found himself the target of two smoldering blue eyes. It was a look both glacial and sultry. Herr Welt smiled feebly and, as earlier, reached to fix his glasses. He looked down, perhaps at her feet, or ankles, she was not sure, but when he looked up, her two jewel-like eyes had widened significantly, as though to express her awareness of his furtive behavior. It was a recriminatory look mitigated by a flirtatious dilation of her dark blue pupils. She did not blink once.

Ursula came out with a small jam jar filled to the top with

brandy, to which she was screwing on the cover. At the same moment, the sirens went off.

Edda fetched some candles from her room, while Ursula went round opening windows. Searchlights swept the sky. Everyone, Herr Werner Welt included, went to the cellar. Annaliese joined them. Lately, Ingeborg had noticed, Annaliese was behaving ever more eccentrically. There was a fugitive look in her eye; she had stopped speaking to others. In the cellar, she sat by herself with a blanket around her and rocked to and fro. Within minutes came the far-off drone of the air formation. Otto Holtzman poured brandy for everyone present, including not only Herr Werner Welt, but both of the children, as well. Ursula appreciated its nutritive value. When Otto brought Annaliese Falke a glass of brandy, she took it in hand without so much as a glance.

To judge by the sound of the flak that commenced going up, the raid was passing over a few miles to the north. There were distinct lulls, too, in the drumming of the antiaircraft guns, during which interludes Ingeborg showed the party block warden an occasional glamorous gaze. Usually when she went into the cellar, she suffered from the distinct horror of being buried alive, which often cast her into a hypnotic and benumbed state of mind. Tonight she felt better. She was sitting opposite Herr Welt at the table where she usually sat reading from one of her books till the all-clear sounded. There was a candle between them. He smiled from time to time.

"I watched you in your garden last summer," she said.

Before Herr Welt could reply, the cellar shook noticeably as the attack over Berlin had begun. Deep tremors radiated beneath them, followed by an echoing of the detonations. The table trembled beneath her hands. She was watching him. She was conscious of the effect of the candle glow on her porcelain features. By now, Herr Welt's admiration of her elfin loveliness was becoming a shared secret. From time to time, Ingeborg sent surreptitious glances toward Edda, Otto, and her mother, at the table in the center of the shelter. Andreas was falling asleep in Ursula's lap; he was sucking his thumb.

"If I had a garden," Ingeborg pointed out, in the way of secretly testing the man from next door, "I would grow nothing but flowers." With that, she lifted her brandy glass to her lips; she watched him cannily.

To her surprise, however, Herr Welt brightened at once and responded with a like sentiment. She had hoped he would argue the obviously sensible course of growing vegetables, so that she could spurn his practical-minded notions.

In the candlelight, Werner Welt's face looked swarthier than before; his eyes loomed large behind his lenses; his hands were stubby and soft. He struck Ingeborg as being of a gentle nature.

"I once had the most beautiful flower garden," he exclaimed. "It was the envy of the neighborhood."

"Under my window?" she came right back.

"I had an arbor, I had trellises, and in the middle of it all a gazebo with a swing in it."

Ingeborg was charmed, and tried to picture her neighbor's yard filled with flowers and pretty furnishings. "Where is everything now?"

"In my cellar, dismantled," he replied.

It pleased Ingeborg to regard the man sitting opposite her as a gardener. "I hope you grew roses," she said pertly.

"I had a world of roses."

"If a garden doesn't have roses," said Ingeborg, stealing a glance in her mother's direction, while maintaining a tone

of ladylike finality, "I would not visit it twice." The pene-
trating look that she then dealt him bespoke her unswerv-
ingness on that point. Herr Welt's fascination with her was
as palpable and apparent to her eye as the man himself. She
was beginning to like him. She liked his ways. She would
have said more, but the table between them began to trem-
ble under her hands. The candle shook violently, its saucer
rattling. A second massive wave of bombers was making for
Potsdam and Berlin. This time, though, Potsdam itself was
hit. The room went dark. Annaliese shrieked from time to
time. When Otto switched on a flashlight, Ingeborg caught a
nightmarish glimpse of Fräulein Falke standing up, clutching her head. Her hair in the beam of light was like that of a
madwoman. Ingeborg was herself terrified. Within a minute, she had squeezed herself underneath her mother on the
cot by the wall. The flak and the crashing of bombs near at
hand was accompanied by the constant sound of glass splin-
tering in the street. She could hear her mother saying "My
babies, my babies," and later recalled that she had called out
for her father in a clear voice, as if he had been in a room
nearby. Smoke was pouring into the cellar. Then came the
cracking report of something structural breaking; ceiling
joists at the back of the cellar snapped in two, several of
them, one after the other, and came down noisily, carrying
floorboards, plaster and lath, a shower of furnishings, and
last of all the piano from the Falkes' parlor.

Later on, Ingeborg's mother got her and Andreas upstairs,
while Edda Holtzman went outdoors in search of rescue
workers. Otto and Werner Welt stayed behind, digging by
flashlight through the mound of debris, trying to get at Annaliese Falke. She was buried under six feet of collapsed
beams and plaster. The house was standing at a severe pitch,
including the floor of their room on the second story. In the

aftermath of the raid, their room was illuminated by the fires from outdoors. Both windows had exploded; the floor was showered with glass. The room was a wreckage: the closet door had burst its hinges, the chest of drawers had fallen forward, and the big porcelain stove was cracked in two. Ingeborg's books lay everywhere.

The view of the sky over Berlin was a crescent of lurid crimson, while three or four houses along the Kanal, two streets away, were burning brightly. The chestnut tree at the corner of Hoditzstrasse was burning like a torch. Ingeborg was crying for a long while. Whenever she got herself under control, the look of mind-stopping confusion on Andreas's face started her crying again.

The body of Annaliese Falke was dug out in the middle of the night and taken away in the early morning on a horse-drawn cart. Otto came upstairs looking sick. Next morning, down in the cellar, he and two workers, using a construction jack, managed to raise up the other side of the house, wedging two fallen beams into place, atop the stone sills, to stabilize the structure. One of the men replaced Ursula's windowpanes. On every street, emergency teams were digging furiously under collapsed houses to get at survivors. A mother and her children were trapped in a cellar on Junkerstrasse all that day, while workers pumped oxygen in, and a collection of bystanders shouted encouragement. Several refugees, it was said, were killed in the open on the grounds of the imperial park. Otto heard from someone that the shortage of coffins was acute, and that many of the dead were being transported out of town to a mass grave.

Ursula and Ingeborg worked all morning to straighten and clean up their house. The windows were replaced, the floor was nearly level, and their bare furnishings were back in place. Electric power was restored around noontime, but an hour later failed again. Ingeborg went alone out to the food shop with money in her pocket and her mother's cards, and stood in a queue by the door. Despite the damage evident along the street, no one on line was talking about the bombing last night. Some of the women, Ingeborg noticed, looked visibly unwell, though. At one point, without warning, an antiaircraft battery north of Potsdam began pounding, and moments later, something momentous, if only for its portentousness of things to come, occurred.

A speedy, low-flying aircraft came whizzing down from the northeast, banked elegantly above the Regierung, and came right down Spandauerstrasse, where Ingeborg and the others were standing. It was a fighter plane. It shot overhead at rooftop level and curved away in the direction of Wannsee and Berlin. Its wings bore Russian markings.

The sight of the Soviet fighter was chilling to all standing on line.

After a silence, a woman spoke up angrily, remarking bitterly on a radio broadcast of the day before by Dr. Goebbels, calling his fulminations "sickening."

"Well, didn't you *know*," remarked an elderly man in a ragged coat, "that they are all mad?"

From behind Ingeborg, a girl of about fifteen wearing a Hitler Youth blouse and scarf under her coat called forward to them in a voice dripping with disgust. "You ought to be locked up, you scum!"

Ingeborg had turned round at the sound of her voice, but

looked back at once. No one spoke. After an anxious pause, the girl, growing angrier, called forward again. "Cowardly scum," she said. "My three brothers died for you!"

That caused Ingeborg a stab of fright. Unaware that her response to the altercation was a replica of her mother's habitual behavior, Ingeborg eliminated from her face any sign of having heard anything. She leafed through the ration cards, rearranging them in her hands, and pretended to be recounting her money. She did not look up. Sometimes when she was alone in public, she felt an unreasonable fear of being arrested and taken away. To worsen things, her waiting in the food queue today proved disappointing, as she went home with nothing more in hand than some butter and radishes.

Everything was breaking down now. People said the national railway system had all but collapsed. There had not been an S-Bahn train to Berlin in thirty-six hours. Ingeborg's school had been closed for a week. The electric power was still off. One day, Ursula came home to say that the war wounded were being evacuated on a large scale, and that her work there had come to an end. "If we can't find work, will we be called up in the Volksturm?" she asked, referring to the "home guard."

"Don't worry about that," Otto replied. "They have no weapons for the so-called Great Levy."

After that, Ursula Maas spent nearly all her time searching for food for her children and herself. On one occasion, she found a kitchen unit of the People's Welfare service set up in the street near the Garrison Church. They were serving sausage, butter, and bread, and a thick delicious soup. Ursula ran home to get her children. They ate in the street, sitting on a stoop on Mammonstrasse. By this time, Andreas was fussing and complaining around the clock. He was worrisomely hungry.

At night, in the dark, Ursula strove to cheer the two of them. She tried daily to hide something away for the two of them to eat, or at least chew away on, in the late evening when she thought they would be getting sleepy. The knowledge that the day would end with something to nibble made the days bearable for them, she thought. Major Paul Frings appeared unexpectedly one evening. He had obviously been very taken with Ursula on the evening they met at Herr Haberzettl's *Weinstube*. He came to their door on this evening looking very correct, the sleeve of his missing arm folded into his coat pocket, his heels together. He carried a parcel of peas, bacon, and white bread.

Ingeborg was touched in her heart by the sight of her mother holding the package of food in her hands and offering the major her sincerest gratitude. A moment later, though, Ursula surrendered to her feelings and did something Ingeborg had rarely seen her do. Ursula broke down. She sat at the table and cried unrestrainedly, her hands to her face. She waved a hand in apology for her behavior.

The army officer shifted uncomfortably on his feet but made no move to comfort her. He was unable, by nature or upbringing, it seemed, to extend himself emotionally. His awkwardness showed.

"I remember you," he said, turning to Ingeborg, in the way of deflecting attention.

"She is my hero," said Ursula, wiping her eyes. "She has more courage and good sense than any soul in Germany, from here to the Alps. I can't imagine being so lucky as to have mothered her." Ursula wept anew. "How did I bear such treasures? . . . Now, I can't even feed them."

Before departing that evening, the major explained that his unit was leaving Potsdam in the morning. "I won't know till then," he said, "whether into Berlin, or west."

Ursula saw him out to the stairway. She wished him luck. "Don't behave foolishly. It's too late for senseless heroism. Even," she added, "for someone who has suffered the losses that I know you have."

At the foot of the stairs, Major Frings looked back and touched the bill of his cap.

"I want you to live," she said.

"Good night," he said.

"Goodbye, Paul."

Ingeborg was disheartened by the return of the letter that she had sent in secret to her father. By an irony, it arrived in the last regular mail delivery. After that day, all postal deliveries came to an end. She had gone out with the pail to the corner pump, and met the carrier on her way back. She went in at the door with the heavy, nearly full pail of water and spotted the letter on the floor. She stopped and picked it up. In all her days, for all her astuteness of mind and character, Ingeborg had probably never reflected in her face such a look of idiocy as occasioned by the envelope in her hand. She gaped at it. Her heart rate slowed to a cold drumming.

She didn't bring the water upstairs, but withdrew to the street. Her heart was oppressed. She made her way over to Hoditzstrasse and turned in toward the Kanal. That was her favorite part of town. The Kanal was very intimate and picturesque, with the walkways on either side of the water, the iron rails, and pretty bridges crossing over it at each street.

Once, there were fish stalls here. There were open-air markets. Leaves from the waterside trees floated sluggishly past. She was oblivious to the freezing air and the sudden icy gusts that whistled under the bridge at Waisenstrasse, by the botanical gardens. The sight of her own handwriting on the envelope to her father, smeared over with the black postal stampings that had sent it back, was repellent to her eye. She turned north past the gardens. In places, the streets were crowded with refugees, as well as soldiers. Going past her school, she scarcely noticed that all the windows were missing. Bits of glass carpeted every street. From one building, where workers had been digging for days, arose the nauseating smell of dead bodies. Ingeborg covered her nose with her mitten. She lost track of time. She went into the chapel that she loved, the one by her school. Today, it held a great throng of people, mostly Russians and Poles, but many German refugees, as well. It was almost warm inside the chapel. There was a constant hum of voices, and the rising sense of panic everywhere was perceptible now.

Soon enough, Ingeborg's thoughts came back into compass, and she realized that her mother would be worried beyond description when she found the bucket of water at the foot of the stairs and no sign of Ingeborg. Before leaving the church, Ingeborg folded the letter in two and stuffed it into the coin box in front of the offertory candles. While striding home, she underwent a spontaneous resurgence of spirit. In fact, she had never been more certain than today, not at any time, that her faithfulness would be borne out. He was alive. She knew it as surely as if he had radioed to her in the night. Turning into Charlottenstrasse, up which came clopping a long column of horses and wagons, she saw it in her mind as clearly as that burned-out chestnut tree up ahead, a railway train coming across a long, wet, dimensionless field. It was swampy there. The train came across the wet plain, with a funnel of gray smoke above it. There were no people to be seen, no houses, or even trees. It was near the ocean. He was aboard the train. It was coming this way.

Otto and Edda Holtzman were talking openly now of their plans to join the flight of refugees headed west. The idea, Otto explained many times, was to get into some unimportant town or village in the west, as close to the front lines as possible, hide out in some barn or cellar, and then be "rolled over," or "rolled around," by the oncoming English or Americans. "We must do that. There is no other safe or sensible thing to do."

"It doesn't sound too safe to me," Edda remarked wryly.

"Berlin and Potsdam will fall to the Russians. I promise you. They're across the Oder. They're less than fifty miles away. What will happen here when that day comes, and it is coming fast, will be a living nightmare. Especially," he added, "for women."

"What about your lady employer?" Edda mocked him playfully. "That's her car you're driving. Are you going to steal it?"

Whenever Otto's loyalty to the von Salmuth-Tresckows was questioned, his air of worldly knowledgeability evaporated on the spot. He stared at Edda incredulously. His mustache bristled. "I am waiting for her to decide when we go," he explained innocently.

Edda set her hand to her head, as in a comic display of disbelief, and looked out the window into the sunlight.

Otto looked from his wife to Ursula, and back again. "I have to take her to safety," he protested.

"And in the meanwhile," Edda came back at him, "we'll all wait till she gives you the sign."

"Naturally," he said.

Edda changed the subject. "This morning he was too tired to get up."

"I'm fifty years old," he reminded her. "I get fatigued."

Edda laughed over that. "At two o'clock in the morning, he has the vigor of a wild stallion. At two in the morning," she lifted her voice, "he could exhaust a hundred women. He's like one of those biblical patriarchs that could beget an entire tribe in one night. But come the dawn," she said, "he can't so much as toast me a biscuit. He's fatigued!"

"I was fatigued," he insisted. "I had a tiresome night."

"You had a tiring night," Edda corrected him.

Ingeborg, who was reading by the window, deduced from the conversation and laughter that Otto and Edda had been doing something of a pleasant and strenuous nature together during the night. She recalled — and it seemed very long ago now — how she and Andreas had had to share her bed the last time her father came home on leave; and she had suspected that time that her mother and father had played intimately after dark in the other bed. That made sense to Ingeborg. She imagined them kissing under the covers. (She wondered, too, what it would be like to kiss Franzi under the blankets. That was an exciting thought, and her mind dwelt upon it for a long moment. Lest anyone read her thoughts, she held her book up in front of her face.)

Before departing, Edda asked Ursula if she would like to bring the two children and stay a few days with Otto and herself in their cottage at Glindowsee.

"I would not do that without official permission. I would

be more frightened to stay out there than to stay here. That's desertion these days. I've heard there are S.S. road-blocks everywhere. Besides," Ursula added, "I'm going to try to find other Red Cross work. I met Dr. Naumann at the Wilhelm Platz streetcar stop, and he said they need help at the train station, where the wounded coming in are being transferred onto trucks."

"It's only another week or so," said Otto, "until every-thing will break down. Then there will be no officials, no lo-cal police, no Gestapo, no S.S. roadblocks. It's coming fast, Ursula. When the day arrives, Edda and I will come for the three of you." He eyed her gravely. "Be ready."

"I am sure you are right." Ursula looked pained.

Later, after the two of them had gone, the electricity was restored for the third time in twenty-four hours. The radio, which came on suddenly, was filled all that afternoon with the most urgent announcements from Berlin, instructing all citizens to resist and destroy the barbaric hordes. At twi-light, the electric power failed once more. Ursula had found a kerosene lamp in Annaliese's house downstairs and used it to heat up their supper, which consisted of codfish and mustard sauce that Edda had secured for them somehow. To Ingeborg, the removal of Edda from her room downstairs to the gardener's house at Glindowsee sharpened the growing sense of isolation and abandonment.

For the next three days, Ursula took her children with her and went in search of food. There were no volunteer street kitchens. At the hospital where she had worked, she was turned away. In a bizarre twist, however, that first day, as the three of them were crossing on foot through the Old Market, crowded with civilians and throngs of rather dusty soldiers, a policeman directed Ursula to take the children for lunch to the Palast Hotel. The hotel was a venerable landmark in Potsdam, very expensive and elegant, just the sort of establishment that had always been beyond the means and aspirations of Ursula. From their table in the dining room, they could see the people flooding past in the broad marketplace beyond the windows. The refugees coming up Humboldtstrasse from the Kaiser Wilhelm Bridge, with their carts and bicycles, some of them dragging bare suitcases on the ground behind them, in an endless stream, looked more exhausted and miserable than any so far. Some of these individuals had been on the road for as much as two months, living in the open all that icy winter, and deriving from as far away as Memelland. Military vehicles coming through the Old Market, blowing their horns, forced everyone out of the way, soldiers and civilians alike.

Ursula was able to order a modest lunch of sausage, bread, and a thin, watery soup. She ate practically nothing herself, wrapping up her own sausage for the children that evening. On the following day, she exchanged a sweater and a pair of shoes that had belonged to Annaliese Falke with a refugee for some flour and rice. In the evenings, however, a time when Ursula had heretofore always been able to generate a warm family feeling, a sense of cold foreboding prevailed. For one thing, the weather stayed bitter. There were no electric lights, no heater, no radio music. With the floor cocked slightly, and their bare furnishings rather ramshackle, it was hard not to be despondent. To conserve candles, mostly they communed in the half darkness. Ursula played records for them. From time to time the unexpected roar from a low-flying fighter plane filled the sky. Ultimately, a night came when Andreas lost the ability to continue. They were sitting at the table. Ursula had heated up and served a soup that had almost no taste. Andreas took one spoonful and put down his spoon.

"I want a potato," he said. He stared into the dim light of the room before him with a setting of his lips which resembled to a remarkable degree his big sister's own best stubborn look. He was trying not to cry. Ingeborg could make out his features clearly from where she sat and divined the seriousness of the moment.

As much as their mother encouraged him, Andreas remained motionless. He stared before himself. Ingeborg noticed the swallowing movements he was making in his throat as he fought back the tears. Ursula lighted a candle at once. She came round and kissed him and urged him again to eat, but the boy was adamant. Ingeborg was moved by the sight of her brother. She had never thought much about her love of Andreas. He was always just a conforming presence, tagging along behind them, or scribbling on something with a pencil. She had forgotten that Andreas had his own war to fight, just as she had hers, and that now he had reached the end of his resources. He had no strength left to fight, nor any more ground to yield. He sat still at the table, wearing two sweaters over his shirt, staring at the candle flame. He insisted on a potato. Looking over these past weeks, Ingeborg realized that Andreas, just six, had, after all, given a good account of himself. That thought set her own eyes burning.

"I'll find something for him to eat," she said.

"Where are you going, Ingeborg?"

"Next door," she replied.

It was the night of the last snowfall of the year. The streets were not only white but unusually silent tonight, as she made her way round the corner to the front door of the party block warden. Two big trolley cars stood dark and empty in the middle of Charlottenstrasse. The snow on Herr Welt's doorstep shone like phosphorus. When he answered her knock, he was astonished to see who it was. To Ingeborg, his warm, cheery greeting came as no surprise. He stepped backward and widened the door.

From the stove-heated sitting room behind him, a wave of warm air pulsed past her. Herr Welt was bundled up, wearing a buttoned cardigan sweater that bulged over his paunch and had on his big-rimmed eyeglasses. He was visibly flattered by her coming to his door. His cheeks shone rosily. While Ingeborg was too young to understand much about the ways and complex dealings of men and women, she was sufficiently astute to recognize and exploit another's admiration of her. In fact, in her cellar on the night of the bad bombing, she had actually imagined that Herr Welt's attitude toward her was probably not so different from the way that Otto looked upon the von Salmuth-Tresckow lady. On entering Herr Welt's house, Ingeborg was thus prepared to play the part of a titled lady paying a visit to her faithful gardener. She recalled the soft, placid, superior expression on that lady's face the day they met and produced a remarkably similar look for the local block warden. What she was not prepared for, however, was the garish interior of the man's sitting room. It was like a candlelit shrine to National Socialism.

On the far wall hung an imposing framed portrait of Adolf Hitler; it was exactly the same as the one on display in the downstairs hall of her school. Smaller framed pictures of other Nazi leaders were located about the room. The doorway leading to rooms at the back was draped with four red and black banners. There were small swastika flags in little holders on various tables. Family pictures stood atop the piano, and above them on the wall a long sepia photo of a World War I military unit, about a hundred men seated shoulder to shoulder, all staring at the camera, one face of which, Ingeborg had no doubt, belonged to the block warden. She felt certain, though, that the effect of the room upon her senses, as both hallowed and garish, was much heightened by the lighting. Two fat candles, one on the piano and one on a table by the inner door, cast a profound glow over everything. After her initial shock, many seconds had elapsed before Ingeborg was able to revive the air of calm gentility that she wished to portray.

"Some of my memorabilia," he muttered, accompanied by a fleeting smile that Ingeborg could not readily decipher. There wasn't a single moment, however, when she feared the man. With her inborn sense of decorousness, she did not immediately come to the point of her visit.

"Where would you like me to sit?" she said, and looked round herself, as though a chair were about to materialize out of thin air.

Quickly, Herr Welt removed a book and newspaper from the cushion of the easy chair near at hand. She was sure it was his own favorite seat, especially after he fetched himself a straight-back chair and sat down upon it close by. Before sitting, she took off her purple coat. Across from her, close to the piano, was an old-fashioned cast-iron stove. Next to it stood a pile of newspapers, cardboard, kindling, and a hod with some coal in it. "Where is Frau Welt?" she asked, but had suspected without ever giving it thought that her neighbor lived alone.

"I have no wife," he said.

"Who is that young woman?" Ingeborg pointed her finger

at a prominent photograph on the left side of the piano. It was the biggest picture on the piano.

"That one?" he signified.

"That one!" Ingeborg pointed a second time and employed a rather curt tone, on purpose, as in showing her impatience with any sort of evasiveness. His obvious desire to please her fueled and colored her responses.

"Her name was Stephanie. I mean," he faltered and corrected himself, "her name is Stephanie, but I don't see her anymore."

Ingeborg grew more adult by the minute. "When did you last see her?"

"That would have been Christmas Day in 1926."

"That's so long ago!" Her instantaneous response carried with it a sophisticated edge suggestive of disapproval. She showed her host a set of startled cobalt blue eyes. She was sitting back with her arms stretched forward along the arms of the big upholstered chair. "Were you planning to be married?" The question was put with the smoothness of an experienced inquisitor having stumbled upon something unexpected. She glanced at Werner Welt from head to foot. A cherry glow from the grate ignited his balding temples; he wore baggy trousers; if he was perspiring faintly, it was probably because her presence in his sitting room made him unsure of himself.

"We were supposed to be," he replied, "but we never were."

"I know you never were," she said a little tartly.

"She underwent a change of mind," he added.

"Were you sorry?"

He was glancing sidelong at the picture on the piano, almost as if he had not examined it in detail in a long while.

His spectacles gleamed and twinkled when he moved his head. Ingeborg was quite sure that the picture on the piano had been enlarged. It looked a little blurry. "Yes, I have always been sorry about that," he admitted.

To Ingeborg the young woman in the picture was ordinary to the point of homeliness. She had a pasty complexion, a smirk that turned her lips, and a rather fleshy chin and neck.

When the man returned his attention to her, Ingeborg got to the point of her call. "My brother is very hungry tonight," she said, "and won't eat his soup. It's very watery. He needs something tasteful."

A look of pain passed through Werner Welt's darkly lighted features. "You," he observed softly, with feeling, "look undernourished."

"Do you have any vegetables left from last summer's garden?"

He had very little to offer. "I'll show you what I have," he said. "It's almost nothing, Fräulein Maas."

He led the way downstairs to his cellar. Ingeborg followed him down the staircase. As concentrated as she was on acquiring something to eat for Andreas, she was enjoying once again the way her middle-aged neighbor showed her such a sedulous respect. Ingeborg had immersed herself in so many books, a hundred romantic storybook worlds, and knew precisely how to comport herself.

"Mostly," said Herr Welt, as he carried one of the big candles at shoulder height, "I have managed to find some rations every day, like everyone else, but most of the time, like everyone else, I'm hungry when I wake up and hungry when I go to sleep."

Ingeborg had no doubt he was telling the truth. She guessed him to be an honest man. In fact, she was certain of it.

In a far corner of the cellar, he showed her the remains of his summer produce, as he opened up the lid of a box that contained a few carrots and a half dozen or so potatoes. "When I have nothing else to eat, I come down here." With that, he proffered Ingeborg two potatoes.

Reaching, Ingeborg took one of them.

"Take both."

"No, thank you."

He had fallen to staring at her through the fan-shaped glow of the candle. She was sure that Herr Welt was a lonely soul who spent much of his time and thoughts in daydreams. She guessed, moreover, shrewdly, that he had been thinking a lot about her lately. He had been thinking about her love of flowers. He had been thinking about the trellises and the arbor and the gazebo, and about great profusions of roses probably. He wanted to grow roses for her. Ingeborg did not disappoint him. With the potato in hand, she looked round into the dark corners and along the cold, shadowy walls of the cellar. "Show me the gazebo," she said.

For five minutes, while Ingeborg held the candle for him, the block warden showed her the dismantled sections of his various garden structures, all neatly stacked along the wall behind the stairway. The number of trellis sections, and of planks and struts and decorative features, was impressive. Ingeborg's manner, while clasping the candlestick, and standing close by his elbow, with her chin up and her lips set concentratedly, was very much supervisory. "What is that called?" She indicated a big acorn-shaped decoration.

"That's the finial, Fräulein. It goes on the very top of the gazebo."

She nodded interestedly. Her vanity was expanding by the

minute. His deference was quite thrilling. Twice, he had addressed her as fräulein. "It's pretty," she said.

"I had it specially lathed by a friend of mine, a woodworker who used to have a shop on the Kanal."

As Ingeborg persisted in her queries and retorts, she was not really playacting any longer. She was thinking about the garden he would plant for her. It was cold in the cellar, and she was eager to get home, but felt drawn to prolonging things. She signified the entire stack of wooden structures with a lateral movement of the candle. "Why did you paint everything dark green?" she inquired.

Herr Welt's face shone ruddily in the candle glow; his eyes were a trifle magnified by the lenses of his glasses; the expression was one of soft intensity. "I didn't want the shape of the bower or the trelliswork to draw attention from the vines and the leaves and the flowers."

While Ingeborg reflected on his reply, which struck her as sensible, she left little doubt that she was uncertain about his aesthetic judgment. For the first time, she was aware that he was awaiting her response. She thought further about it.

"Should it be white?" he said, finally.

The wonderful feeling inside her which Herr Welt's infatuation created did not blind her to the fact that she liked the man very much, and she knew that he wanted her to reject the green paint. "I think," said Ingeborg, at last, "that the gazebo should be white — and if the gazebo is white, then everything should be white."

Her neighbor nodded resignedly over the wisdom of her words, as though the girl had settled a point of enduring controversy within him. "I'm going to paint it white."

"I would like that," said Ingeborg.

On the way upstairs, while thanking him, Ingeborg addressed him as Herr Welt.

"You may call me Werner," he said.

"I will," she said. She gave him the candle at the top of the stairs. He helped her get her things and held her coat for her. Ingeborg recalled a remark that Anna Freytag once made about Herr Welt, whom she knew from her Saturday political meetings. She said the block warden was not equal even to his own lowly position in the party. She said he was simple. Ingeborg did not think he was simple. She thought him lonely and innocent.

While buttoning her coat, she crossed to the piano and looked at the World War I picture on the wall above. She wanted Werner Welt to know that she took a personal interest in his past life. He pointed to himself in the picture. His was the third face in the third row. Ingeborg examined his face at close range. He was waiting for her to react. Ingeborg made a soft throaty sound and stepped back a bit, still regarding the picture with a blank, judicious expression.

"You were just a boy," she said. "You were nice-looking, Werner."

She turned to see how he would respond to her employing his first name.

He nodded pleasurably. "We were all boys."

Before she left, he tried to press upon her the other potato. He had it in his hand. The sight of it made Ingeborg's mouth water. For days now, her hunger was never more than one thought away from the center of her mind. But she waved it away.

"Thank you for what you gave me," she said.

"Would you like to come back this Sunday and talk about your garden?"

"Sunday is Easter," Ingeborg reminded him.

"Maybe Monday," he said.

Ingeborg reflected briefly. "Yes," she said. "I'll come Monday."

"We could plan the garden." He was standing beside her at the door. "We could plan it on paper."

"Where everything will go," said Ingeborg, with a nod. She was pulling on her gloves. Herr Welt opened the door for her. Ingeborg showed him an icy smile and stepped outdoors. He followed a step or two, and peered out through the dropping snowflakes to where the two big trolley cars were standing dark and silent on Charlottenstrasse. As Ingeborg headed toward the corner with her head down, he called good night to her.

"Good night, Werner," she answered.

Ingeborg had been gone about thirty minutes, but when she came back upstairs, Andreas remained pouting at the table. He looked both childish and babylike; she watched later as he forked pieces of fried potato into his mouth, like a little prisoner concentrated on the most elemental of pleasures. Ingeborg guessed that he would not be able to pretend any longer that he was not needful of special care. He had to be babied now. She saw it in the way his eyes glistened wetly and avoided looking up, as he chewed on the hot, salted potato slices.

While the boy was eating, the lights and radio came on suddenly. The room in which they lived looked especially derelict now. The floor was still pitched to some extent; the closet door was gone; the tall porcelain stove, which was cracked, stood tilted to one side, like an ancient person gone lame. Ingeborg had thought their living circumstances here to be very reduced compared to those early halcyon days in

Berlin; but now, she saw that the life they had known here during these past two years — while she was still going out eagerly to school every morning, and sitting to a warm supper at night, reading, watching her mother iron or bathe Andreas in the galvanized tub — had been cozy, after all. For the first time in memory, Ingeborg had stopped reading. Probably for want of adequate nourishment, she couldn't reconstruct the world behind the printed page. Her hunger left her light-headed. She was becoming uncharacteristically listless. Once or twice, without thinking what she was doing, she sat in her mother's lap, with her knees drawn up.

By now, the world of the pretty pink-curtained apartment on Fasanenstrasse, where her father smoked his pipe and read the newspaper while her mother made cake frosting, was more remote and fantastic to her mind and heart than the faraway fictional green fields of olden times, where handsome jousting knights once capered to and fro.

April was a tribulation. The streets were crammed, all day and much of the night, not only with the swelling mass of civilian traffic, with automobiles, bicycles, even horse-pulled carts, and columns of refugees headed northwest on foot toward Lübeck and Hamburg, but with soldiers and military vehicles moving through to the front. It was rumored that German units in the west, especially those facing the British, were now giving ground intentionally, while units east of Berlin were fighting doggedly to stem the Russian onslaught. Locally, control posts had been established to forestall a complete breakdown of order. Streetcars stood idle in the city, while nearly all outside railway communication had been severed. In Potsdam, gas and electric power were limited to two hours a day. The shops were all empty and closed. Ingeborg's mother had found work nearby, on Wilhelm Platz, in a Red Cross distribution center. Whenever the siren wailed, she came running home at once.

On one occasion, Ingeborg saw some fifteen-year-old boys whom she recognized go hurrying past in the street. They were carrying shovels, but one or two of them had rifles, and another a panzerfaust. They were members of the Volksturm who had been called up. One of them was Hansi Heiss, Bübchen's younger brother. On another day, when she was at the corner water pump, Ingeborg saw two other familiar boys go past in stiff new Wehrmacht uniforms. The sight of them struck her as ridiculous. They looked like actors in a school play.

The weather was wet and drizzly much of the time now. The temperatures were up; winter was breaking. Night after night, Ursula and the children sustained themselves on the barest of rations, often consisting of peanut butter and bread. Andreas suffered from diarrhea and fussed over it. Ursula took him one morning to an elderly doctor who lived close by and was doing his best to help those in need. While they were gone, Ingeborg put a record on the wind-up phonograph and spent a few minutes doing some chores. Hearing the report of a door shutting in the yard below, she went to the window in time to see Werner Welt stepping outdoors. He did not chance to look up. He was shaking out a blanket. At that moment, the yard lit up with sunlight, and the sun ignited the crown of his half-bald head. The last time Ingeborg had called at his door, the block warden was not home. She had not spoken to him since the night more than a week ago when he had shown her the arbor and trellis latticework in his cellar. In the five minutes to follow, Ingeborg surrendered to a childish impulse.

She had hidden Betka von Stutterheim's gift to her of the suede makeup pouch behind the books stacked under her bed. She had not opened it once since that disappointing day when Betka had moved away to Ulm. In no time, Ingeborg had the makeup case in hand and was sitting in front of the wall mirror; she emptied the pouch of its tubes, brushes, and powders, and prepared to make herself a face. Werner, she was sure, was the only person in existence who would be able to appreciate what she was about to do. In fact, he would be flattered. She worked delicately with the tiny applicator brushes. Twice, she wiped away some mascara and started again. Twice, she removed the lilac hue from her eyelids, in order to redo and soften the effect. The lipstick she applied was as subtle as the blush of nature itself; it was barely noticeable but provided the magical final touch. Going out, Ingeborg did not forget to bring a damp hand towel, with which, later, before returning home, she could wipe it all away.

Underneath her coat, she was wearing the priceless hand-embroidered Czech blouse that Otto had given her, and her black patent shoes. She kept her head down when she entered the street. The sun was still shining as she turned the corner into Jägerstrasse and knocked forcefully on the block warden's door. If Ingeborg Maas knew nothing else, she knew that the man within would be much gratified by the sight of her on his step. She heard him undoing the chain lock and waited for him to open the door, with an artful expression on her lips, friendliness tempered with the reserve of a kindly and liberal-minded superior.

"Fräulein!" The block warden's face lighted.

Ingeborg stepped past him into the house at once, as she did not wish to be seen with her makeup on by anyone in the street. Still, she did want her friend Werner to notice her beautiful look, and regarded him therefore very candidly at close range once inside. "Hello, Werner," she exclaimed. "I hope you are not busy." Her eyes sparkled prettily. "I have come about the garden."

Herr Welt was so surprised by her visit that he seemed nonplussed momentarily. He wrung his pudgy hands, and looked round this way and that, as though he had left something on the floor behind him. Even before he replied, Ingeborg knew by instinct that whatever he was about to utter would contain some polite, self-effacing sentiment. She was not disappointed.

"I must apologize," he said, "for not having been here on Monday."

"That was a week ago Monday," she corrected him, with a playful pertness, while at the same time showing him again her makeup.

"Yes," he admitted. "I was ordered to spend the evening at a meeting of the Price Controls Board. There was not a way I could notify you. . . . I would not know how to do that, anyway," he added, giving word to the secret nature of their friendship.

Ingeborg felt a physical pleasure at the way Herr Welt was acknowledging her importance. He was like one of those loyal retainers in days of old who treated the young lady of the castle with a fawning solicitude that exceeded the manners and formalities even of romantic love. It was delightful, too, to continue to show him her cool, shell pink face. She knew he had noticed. She took off her coat. The instant that Werner Welt made a motion to take it from her, she dealt it to him with a flourish. "Thank you, Werner."

"In peacetime," he said, doubtless alluding to what she might expect of him in future, "that sort of interruption would not arise."

Ingeborg said nothing to that, but could not conceal from her eyes the effects upon her vanity of his honeyed words. She knew he was not joking, either. He was very devoted to her and would have spared nothing in making her the most beautiful garden in all of Potsdam. This realization made it only easier for Ingeborg to preen a little.

For the remainder of her visit, the warden played the role of the honored host while Ingeborg sat on the piano bench, her back straight, her skinny legs folded aslant, and her hands clasped tightly on her lap. Had an impartial third party been present to observe the two of them in secret, there could be no doubting the pathos of the picture they formed. There was a rosy hue in Werner Welt's cheeks as he treaded softly about trying to please and spoil the girl. He was visibly enchanted by her visit. If Ingeborg, seated primly amid the garish collection of Nazi symbols and memorabilia, pre-sented Herr Welt with the smiling, self-collected air of a young lady of high descent, the stoutish middle-aged bache-lor was motivated only that much more to indulge her. He put a big picture book of flowers and flower gardens on the oak center table, and next to it a pretty Meissen plate with two biscuits. He showed Ingeborg a half-full bottle of cognac he had had on hand for a year and kept on a low shelf in a cabinet by the door. "Are you permitted to drink cognac?"

"Oh, yes, it's very nutritious."

Werner Welt set out two small glasses, filled them, set the bottle nearby, and put two straight chairs at the table. They seated themselves opposite one another. Several times, as Ingeborg turned the pages of the big gardening book, he came round from his chair and looked over her shoulder. Ingeborg ate her biscuit in small bites, and sipped her cognac from time to time, while turning the big colorful pictures and remarking on what she saw. Before long, Herr Welt had stopped sitting down altogether and stood by her side.

"Where did the gazebo used to be?" she wished to know.

"It was in the middle of the garden."

"Is that where you are planning to have it?" she asked, turning her head only partially in putting the question.

"That would depend," he answered.

Ingeborg was very businesslike and precise in expressing herself, very much the young lady of affairs. She turned a page, paused, and again half-turned her head. "Depend upon what?"

He made no effort to conceal his feelings. "On where you want it," he said. "I'll put it where you want it."

She liked that response very much! In fact, it inflamed her ego. She showed him her sapphire eyes. "I would like it to be in the sunniest part of the garden."

"That would be by the back wall."

She looked back at the book and reached to turn the page. "That's where I want it."

"It will be a wonderful place for you to read your books." The block warden's swarthy face mirrored the doting affection he felt for his little neighbor.

"Werner," she spoke up, her vanity mounting, "why don't you show me the garden space." With that, she closed the book with the formality of a priest shutting a Bible and got to her feet. Werner led the way out of the sitting room to the back door. The yard was sunlit. From the street beyond the brick wall came a steady shuffling of passersby on foot punctuated by the squeaking of cart wheels. Ingeborg and Herr Welt appeared oblivious to the somber echoes of refugees on the move. Ingeborg glanced up at her own window, which glittered darkly on the upper story.

"Where did you have the arbor?" she wished to know.

"Right here," he replied, "above the door."

"Oh, that's the perfect place for it!" Ingeborg's spontaneous reaction, laden as it was with praise from on high, did more than anything prior to this time to cast her friend in the role of the anxious-to-please employee. "It's exactly where I want it." She gestured. "Covered with flowers."

"With roses, Fräulein?"

"Hundreds," said Ingeborg. "Pink ones."

"Pink would be best."

"And there'll be pathways." She turned to the yard. "And you have benches. Is that," she said, pointing, "the sunniest spot?"

"It is."

Ingeborg sucked in her lips while surveying the muddy, wall-enclosed yard. It was quite spacious, big enough for a flower garden of very gracious proportions. She could see it in her mind's eye. There would be lilac trees and forsythia, flower beds and flowering shrubs, with pebbled pathways winding among them. Sometimes, too, she imagined, Werner would show her about of a morning, pointing out for her satisfaction the plantings and prunings and such that he had most recently done for her.

Ingeborg did not wish to remain outdoors any longer,

however, as Ursula might return at any moment and see her from their upstairs window. She had not forgotten for one second about the makeup, nor was she insensible to the fact that makeup was all but taboo these days, even for adults. Her mother would be thunderstruck. But while still outdoors, in the full sunlight, she could not resist making sure that her neighbor had appreciated her glamorous preparations, and at the last moment yielded to childish promptings. "Did you notice, Werner," she said, "that I am wearing makeup?" She widened her eyes as though to challenge his sensitivity to such things.

He stared at her from behind his dark-framed spectacles.

"It's French," she said, and moved her face laterally without altering her glance.

A moment elapsed. Werner Welt blinked repeatedly. "You're very beautiful, Fräulein."

"Is *that*," she inquired in a clipped voice, but not without humor, "why you want to make me a garden?"

Although the block warden was perhaps obtuse, or at least a lonely and obsessive man of ordinary abilities, he responded nonetheless diplomatically. "I think, Fräulein Maas, it is because you're smarter than other people."

That pleased her visibly, as she turned and entered the back door of the house. A sudden roar from overhead of six German fighter planes coming down from Mecklenburg, and headed south of Potsdam, drew no reaction from either of them. "If there's enough light in the cellar," she said, "I'd like to see again some sections of the gazebo. First, I'll need my coat. I'm getting cold."

A minute or two later, in the basement, Ingeborg began feeling teary. Maybe it was the cold dampness of the cellar that caused it, or Werner's solicitude in bringing down her coat; or it might have found a deeper cause. Ingeborg had

lived all her childhood in a world that was running backward; a world that proceeded from the greater happiness to
the lesser, from small sadnesses to big ones, from the modest comforts of yesterday to hardship, growing deprivation,
ruin in the streets. While Werner bolted together two sections of his gazebo, he was unaware that Ingeborg Maas was
watching him with glistening eyes. Her mind was elsewhere, focused on the one stable point amid the ever-growing worry. She was wondering if her father still carried her
picture folded into his paybook. She wondered whether
there were men with him who loved him and helped to keep
him safe. What troubled her most of all right now was her
knowledge that a day was coming soon when Otto and Edda
would come with a car to their apartment next door, and all
would be made ready for them to leave, and that she, Ingeborg, on that day, would have to tell her mother that she
was not leaving. If Ingeborg's resolution in that regard was
unconscious until now, today it took form in the front of
her mind. Because if she ever left their house next door, she
would never see her father again. That was a certainty. He
would never find her. It was her staying in place, her waiting
for him, that would bring him home. Every fiber and cell of
her being contributed to that conviction. From here, he
went away. To here, he would return.

Werner noticed that Ingeborg was crying. He was peeking
at her through one of the diamond-shaped openings of a trellis. "Why are you crying?" he asked.

She was touched as well by her neighbor's kindness, the
sight of him bolting together sections of the gazebo for her.
She had set her hand to her face in a distracted manner.
"You're very nice to me, Werner," Ingeborg said.

❖

Ursula Maas had a horror that the house they lived in, having collapsed in part the night Fräulein Falke was killed, was unsafe now and could not withstand another violent bombing. The idea of their taking refuge in the cellar of the rectory originated with Ingeborg. Going by herself across the street, Ingeborg tried the front door and found it open. Except for some of the big, ponderous pieces of furniture in the parlor, the house was empty from top to bottom. Ingeborg came back at once to fetch her mother. Ursula had found it hard to believe that no one had moved in, given the plight of so many people. She was leading Andreas by the hand.

Ingeborg had her own theory. "Nobody wants to stay, Mommy. I think by now there are other empty houses in Potsdam."

"You are probably right."

"Everyone is talking about Holstein. The refugees in the street are saying they are going there." Ingeborg was secretly sounding her mother on the subject of leaving. "Where is Holstein?"

"It's in the north."

"Is that where the British are?"

"I think that's true," said Ursula.

They were inside the house, looking into the kitchen and other downstairs rooms. To Ingeborg, the kitchen looked very desolate, as it was here that she had spent many pleasant winter afternoons with Anna Freytag. While most of the windows of the house had been left ajar to protect the glass from the air pressure of explosions, the kitchen windows were blown in. The floor sparkled with the showered glass. Upstairs, Betka's books were still in the bookcase, and the mattress of her bed rolled up atop the springs. The vanity at which Betka sat looked forlorn and filled Ingeborg with feelings of unhappiness over her vanished friend.

The cellar of the rectory was quite dark, but big and clean. Three wicker chairs and a table lay scattered about the floor. The great stones of the ancient foundation were reassuring to the eye.

"It was very wise of you to suggest this cellar," Ursula complimented her daughter.

"Yesterday, Mommy, at the trolley stop, someone said that the enemy bombings will stop soon, because their own soldiers are too close."

"I don't know what to say to that," said Ursula. She opened a big door and looked up the back steps into the yard behind the rectory. Except for a charred tree, the yard was empty. The narrow band of sky showing above the backs of the houses that faced the Kanal was very blue. Again, Ingeborg tested her mother on the subject of leaving.

"I think, Mommy, we would be all right to stay right here at home, even if Edda and Otto and the others do go away."

"We'll see when the time comes," Ursula let fall, as she shut the door.

In the meanwhile, Andreas had made a discovery of his own. He found a chess set in a box on a dusty ledge by the stairs, and, on opening it, thrilled to the pretty wooden figures inside, especially the little white and black horses. Ursula told him that he could take it with him. Lately, Ingeborg's love of Andreas was becoming more conscious to her mind, and she was touched by the sweet look of joy on his face as he carried the box up the cellar stairs. She was not unmindful that her little brother had known nothing in all his days but the alerts, the cold room, the hunger, the night after night of living in fear of the crashing bombs. He expected nothing else and was filled with childish excitement over his momentary good luck with the chess set. He hadn't dreamed that his mother would tell him he could keep it for himself.

"Wasn't Andreas lucky to have found such a beautiful game?" said Ingeborg, diplomatically, as the three of them crossed the trolley tracks to their house.

"Yes, he was."

Andreas showed them a foxy look over his shoulder as he led the way up the stairs to their room. In the remaining hour before darkness, Ingeborg drew a perfect checkerboard on the back of their kitchen-table oilcloth, and, as best she could, showed Andreas how to marshal the chess pieces. The late sun from the street window lighted up Andreas's face, as he sat at the table, bundled in sweaters, looking unusually proud of himself.

Four hundred miles to the west, the Lancasters and Mosquitos coming down from three separate airfields in England began converging over the waters somewhere east of Norwich. As the bombers gained steadily in altitude, climbing to stratospheric heights, the setting sun at twilight appeared to be re-emerging from the sea. The long train of bombers wheeled slowly eastward. The target for tonight was not Hamburg, or Berlin, or any of the cities of the interior. The target was Potsdam itself. Tonight, within hours, the venerable garrison town would be blasted and set burning from one end to the other. The British turret gunners, with nothing of an important or deadly nature yet to do, basked in the evening sun.

3

WHEN THE SIRENS SOUNDED, and the three
of them hurried outdoors and across the darkened street to
the rectory, Andreas brought his chess box. Ursula carried a
packed suitcase, in the event of their inability to return
home, along with blankets, candles, and a flashlight. Ingeborg carried the big jar of tea and the crackers that Ursula
brought home from work. Searchlights, coming up from Babelsberg and the Potsdam Forest, swept the sky. As always,
the firing of the flak batteries was heavy. The air in the cellar of the rectory vibrated to the steady pounding. Presently, the vanguard of a formidable air formation came
droning; the sound was awesome, deadly, irresistible. As
the planes flew overhead, the roar was indescribable; it was
deafening, as though endless freight trains were running
through on the floor above their heads. Everything shook
violently when the first bombs crashed down on the historic district nearby. Whole trees were thrown across the
streets adjacent to the Lustgarten. Within minutes, the famous little city erupted in fires. Both Ingeborg and Andreas
had crawled into their mother's lap; they were kneading
her flesh with their hands. In fact, for the first time during
the war, Ingeborg lost all her self-control. The three of
them were bucked from the chair on which Ursula was
holding them; Ingeborg leaped up from the cement floor
and ran this way and that, clutching her ears and scream-

ing. The bombs came whistling down. With each crash, the three of them cried out.

From outdoors came the wailing of fire engines. Suddenly, the cellar door blew in. Torn from its hinges, the door flew across the cellar and hit the stairs. The cellar lighted up red. The outdoors was aglow. All the houses along the Kanal were burning brightly. Smoke billowed in from the yard. Ingeborg's mother was shouting for her. In that instant, a red incendiary flare danced evilly past the doorway with a magnificent hissing. At the height of the attack, the detonations merged into a single upending blast that went on and on. There, in the hellish light of the basement, the wicker chairs were jigging and waltzing about the floor, as though directed by a supernatural force. Ingeborg gave out a shriek when she saw Andreas break free of his mother's grasp and dart across the flame-brightened room. The expression on his face was unearthly. He was crying and slapping the cellar wall with the flats of his hands. "Make them stop! Make them stop!" When Ursula got to him, Andreas had passed into a state of shock. The little boy's hair was actually standing on end. His mouth was open, his eyes wide as saucers.

Outside, a shower of building stones came down in a noisy hail. The air temperature in the room was rising fast. At one moment, an immense ball of flame, connected to nothing, came traveling past the open door, rose and hovered above the yard, like a flaming beast hatched from the growing conflagration, searching for something combustible. To Ursula Maas, lying on the floor atop her two children, the fateful hour had come. There was no question in her mind about it. It was the end of the world.

A half mile away, Burgstrasse was a river of fire. It was

ablaze from one end to the other, with every building down, and a sky-high pillar of smoke mixed with flame arising from the Church of the Holy Spirit. The most renowned structures, like the town palace and St. Nicholas's Church, were taking direct hits. A man blown from his house directly into the street, and caught up in a great suck of hot wind, tumbled like a sack of rags up Kaiserstrasse. He threw himself somehow full-length into the icy waters of the Kanal. All of Potsdam was burning. When, finally, the drone of the Lancasters began to fade, in the aftermath, high winds were bursting through the streets. The streets were lighted as bright as day. All night long, the sound of a hundred crackling blazes combined into a single roar. The undersides of clouds shone with a sickly pink.

After the all-clear sounded, Ingeborg emerged with her mother and brother into Charlottenstrasse; all three were visibly distressed. Ursula led them by the hand. The sky was aglare. Clouds of smoke moiled upward from burning ruins. Citizens hurried past with pale, stricken faces. Their own house was still upright and intact, but the devastation up and down the street was all but incomprehensible to the senses. The world from which they had sought refuge just hours ago, the familiar trees and landmarks, the streets and houses, was fallen and burning. Entire collections of houses were gone. In places, as at the head of Hoditzstrasse close by, the rubble of masonry and stone was ten feet deep. All the streets of Potsdam were impassable to vehicles. Now and again, from one quarter or another, came a delayed mine explosion that set everything rocking again. The city was shattered.

Upstairs, scarcely conscious of what she was doing, Ingeborg washed Andreas's face; there was a deadened light in his eyes, as he let her minister to him; he continually licked his lips; a tinny sound escaped his throat with every breath. The glare of the burning city illuminated the room fully with a crimson flickering. When Ursula told Ingeborg that she was going outdoors to help in the rescue of people who had been wounded or trapped, Ingeborg understood.

Together, they covered Andreas with two blankets.

"You'll be all right," Ursula told her. "I'm going out to help, but I won't be far away."

Ingeborg heard the sound of her mother going down the front stairs. In fact, within four or five minutes, Ingeborg was herself fast asleep in her bed.

All the next day, which was a Sunday, throngs of people toiled to extricate the living and to recover the dead from collapsed buildings. In Ingeborg's neighborhood, the ruins of the high school on the Kanal were used as a collection point for the unidentified dead. On the Kanal, near Wilhelm Platz, a streetcar stood on its roof, its wheels in the air, like the exoderm of a fabulous insect. Ursula and another woman had found a supply of tea at the distribution center and had set up their own relief station by the Kanal, doling cups to rescue workers. Ingeborg and Andreas were kept busy washing and rinsing. By afternoon, many people who had prudently hoarded, or stored from sight, some few skimpy food supplies in recent weeks, found themselves bringing their treasures out to Ursula's station by the Kanal. Ingeborg was filled with pride over her mother's selfless, efficient presence on the scene, by the way she had improvised and organized her relief station out of nothing. By twilight, Ursula was actually dispensing bread, butter, and bits of sausage, along with the cups of hot tea. To everyone coming and going, she was the smiling soul of helpfulness. Ursula told no one, nor probably thought consciously of it herself, but her heart was brimming with feelings of thankfulness that her children were well and intact nearby; that God had gifted them another day; that the sun was shining in the sky. She couldn't walk past Ingeborg or Andreas without running the flat of her hand lovingly over their heads, giving them a pat. Long after dark, having accumulated by then two or three helpers, Ursula was still running her field kitchen by the Kanal.

When Ingeborg complimented her mother late that night on all that she had done that day, Ursula replied with characteristic humility. "It's all I know how to do," she said.

"I think it's more than that," said Ingeborg, trying that evening to emulate her mother, first by sweeping up the window glass from the floor of their room, by working with her mother by candlelight to tack up the draperies where the windows used to be, and chattering away on a dozen subjects. She was inexpressibly proud of Ursula. She was happy to notice, also, that Werner Welt's house stood intact across the way.

"I feel most badly for the Potsdamers," Ursula observed, "people who have lived here all their lives, and last night saw it all destroyed at a stroke. So many beautiful buildings. Do you remember the swans on the Havel last summer?"

"Yes, I do."

"With the rowboats going by the town palace."

"It's all gone now," said Ingeborg.

"But I," said Ursula, "have always known that we would not live here after the war."

"We won't," said Ingeborg, who had some very definite ideas about the future.

During the night, a wind came up, followed by a spring rainstorm, with the wind blowing the cold rain in sheets. Ingeborg awoke to the noise of the wind shaking the draperies and the rain splashing on the windowsills and floor. Their one-room apartment was a ruin now. But like her mother, Ingeborg felt somehow less despondent, having survived the massive bombing of the night before. Rising, she went in her stocking feet and peeked out the front window to the street. Wet smoke trickled up from the demolished building next door to the rectory. The rooftop of a wrecked automobile glistened in the rain. Ingeborg remained at the window for a very long while.

In all Potsdam, probably Ingeborg Maas alone stood witness that night to the opening of the final Soviet assault on Berlin. The sky to the east shone clear, when, beyond the fallen dome of St. Nicholas's Church, the distant heavens lit up with color. She was watching, when, a second later, north of that, the sky took on a general purple glow. There was no sound, not an echo, of the tremendous barrage that had just commenced all along the Oder, just the display of purple lights, as more than five thousand Russian artillery pieces opened fire along a sixty-mile front. In her heart, Ingeborg divined its importance. There was something both beautiful and apocalyptic about it.

Next day, the air space over Berlin was swarming with Russian aircraft. In Berlin, for the first time in nearly six years of war, the word "front" attained a visible significance: the swirling hornetlike fighter planes; the earth shaking round the clock from the artillery; and the frightening knowledge that beneath and behind the planes and artillery lights in the east, like something hellish in its destructive power, like an oncoming natural cataclysm, came the ar-

mored ground machine, crushing and smashing the life out
of everything before it. The front was a killing zone, grinding across the landscape with tidal inexorability.

Everyone was bolting. Being in the midst of the only remaining escape corridor from Berlin, Potsdam saw a further
swelling of refugee traffic. Ingeborg would not have thought
there were so many people in all the world, as they pushed
through to the west by the hundreds, even thousands. They
came on foot all the way from Kurstin, Frankfurt on the
Oder, and points east. Stalled cars were pushed to one side.
All railroad traffic had come to a stop. One afternoon, she
saw in the distance several dozen figures making their way
single-file across the damaged railroad bridge that spanned
the Havel just south of town, looking like a string of black
insects. That was the day, as it happened, of the last daylight raid on Berlin; the last appearance ever of the high-fly-
ing American bombers coming on in formation, a silvery ar-
mada of planes twinkling ominously in the sun.

Friday morning, when Ingeborg was coming back from
the corner pump with a pail of water, she heard a bumping
sound in the Falkes' apartment, set down her bucket, and
looked in. She recoiled in surprise. A man whom she had
never seen before was standing at the back of the room
calmly buttoning his shirt. Ingeborg knew at once what he
was doing, though; a closet door stood open behind him, and
on the floor at his feet lay his own clothing in a pile. It was
an S.S. uniform. He smiled at her. He appeared quite cheerful, in fact. He was going matter-of-factly through the mo-
tions of putting on Dr. Falke's civilian clothing. "Good
morning, Fräulein," he said, as he came past her, pulling on
his suit jacket and tugging at his lapels, and went blithely
out the front door. Ingeborg watched from the doorstep

as he strode out to the crowded street and lost himself among the people thronging past.

At Wilhelm Platz that noon, just after Ingeborg had taken Andreas to meet their mother, and had told her about the S.S. man putting on Dr. Falke's clothing, Ingeborg spotted a man strolling across the park, and knew she had seen him somewhere before. Then she remembered. He was the man who owned the restaurant on Zeppelinstrasse. His name was Felix Haberzettl. Today, he was dressed very sportily, offering an oddly flamboyant picture amid the devastation. He wore a soft hat with a green feather in the band, a tweedy brown hunting jacket with suede elbow patches, and spats showed under the cuffs of his trousers. Striding toward them along the bluestone walk, swinging the tip of his umbrella before him, he recognized Ingeborg as the pert little lady whom he had seated by the fire on Christmas Eve. Pausing, he touched the brim of his hat in the way of greeting Ursula.

"You," he remarked to Ursula, "are the mother of my favorite and most illustrious patron."

"Oh, yes." Ursula brightened over his words. "I am becoming best known for that. As the mother of Ingeborg."

The restaurateur nodded. "I once knew a lady named Ingeborg. She came from the Arctic Circle."

Ingeborg showed the florid-faced man a pretty smirk. She liked being teased.

"I am speaking the truth," he said. "May my honor depend on it. She was beautiful beyond my powers of description, and quite rich into the bargain. She owned immense herds of reindeer. You don't believe me," he said to Ingeborg.

"I do not," Ingeborg piped back, flashing her eyes at her

mother. Compressing her lips, she looked away to left and right.

"If you saw her on the snowy evening she came to my restaurant, you would have. She wore a reindeer hat, a reindeer coat, and reindeer gloves and boots."

"Did she ride upon a reindeer?" Ingeborg replied without a moment's reflection, her expression that of disbelief tempered by patience.

"Nobody believes me," he said. "She sat in the choicest chair at my choicest table, surrounded by a dozen little dwarves in reindeer cloaks, and sipped champagne till dawn."

Ursula could not resist a joke of her own. "I am afraid," she said, "that those days are gone forever."

"If what we are seeing all about us is a sign of things to come, an idiot would readily agree." He signified the scorched trees and fallen buildings with a sweep of his umbrella.

"Were you hurt badly by the bombing?" Ursula wished to know.

"I stand before you," he responded, almost heartily.

"Your restaurant."

"My restaurant, it grieves me to report, has become the memory of a restaurant. I wonder if ever so many things were ever so rapidly made into memories."

In the midst of the shattered city, with people eddying past them with frazzled and sleepless expressions, Herr Felix Haberzettl was an isle of moral repose. The ground underfoot trembled all the while from the artillery bombardment falling now and incessantly inside Berlin proper.

Ursula put a question to Felix that she would not have conceived posing in the past. She was sincerely curious on the point. "Are you planning to leave Potsdam?" she asked.

"Ach," he said, with a movement of his head, as though to confront once more a persisting irritant. He pondered it momentarily. "I think," he responded, "I will not go. After all, why should I?"

Ingeborg's heart leaped on hearing his response. Until now, she had lacked the moral strength to tell her mother that she was not leaving, either. By now, Ingeborg was convinced to the roots of her being that it was her waiting for him that would bring her father home. On that point, her faith was unimprovable. Betka may have run away; and the man putting on a suit of clothes this morning in Dr. Falke's house may also have run away; and Otto and Edda would soon pack up and leave. But Ingeborg was not leaving, and would never yield, no matter what; because everything that there was on earth depended on that. If she went away, if they went by car or on foot out west of the summer palace, leaving Potsdam behind, and their dismal house empty on Charlottenstrasse, it was as certain to her as the sun and moon that the figure of the soldier walking home along silent roads would vanish like smoke in the air, like a thought, and be gone forever.

"After all," Herr Haberzettl was saying, "if *I* haven't the right or reason to be here, who should? I was born at Number 10 Mammonstrasse. I worked as a boy not a hundred feet from there, in the kitchen of the Hotel Deutsches Haus. This is where I live. As a child, I could have walked the streets of the city blindfolded. Now," he said, "that is precisely what we are all doing."

With that, Herr Haberzettl smiled and bowed his head, and set off, resuming his leisurely stroll amid the sunlit wreckage.

❖

When the time arrived for Ursula and her children to depart Potsdam with Otto and Edda, Ingeborg could not quell the shaking in her stomach. It came to pass in the early morning. Ursula was getting ready for her day's work at the Red Cross center, when the Holtzmans came up the stairs. Otto's employer, Berenice von Salmuth-Tresckow, had actually obtained official permits for all of them, he said.

While Otto explained himself, Ingeborg stood with her back to the window that overlooked Werner Welt's garden. She was frightened by the look of the permit that he held in his hand, fearful that it amounted to some form of government order that could not be ignored. She had not anticipated such an eventuality. Her heart was racing.

"The end is fast approaching," Edda interrupted to say.

"I hope you are right about that," said Ursula, who looked truly bewildered this morning, as though she had lost the capacity to grapple with what was unfolding. As Otto and Edda told her what she must do, she glanced nervously from one to the other, and then round at her children. She wrung her hands. She was trying to understand.

"With luck," Otto continued, "we'll be in the vicinity of Lübeck in a matter of hours. In the next two or three days, you may trust me, our forces are going to *give* Lübeck to the British." He showed Ursula the signature on the official permit. "That information comes from Admiral Semler himself. Believe me, it is going to happen! And we are going to be there. All six of us."

Ursula Maas's lack of worldliness was made plain in her subsequent question. "We are going into captivity?"

Otto pointed out the window behind which Ingeborg was standing, in the direction of Berlin, where actual street fighting had been going on for six days now. The noise was constant. "Edda was right, Utsie. It's coming fast. There can be no question of your staying here."

"Well —" Ursula looked about herself in confusion, as though some familiar object would shed an elucidating light.

"You may take only one bag with you," Otto instructed her. "We don't want to put anything on the roof of the car that would indicate we're refugees or fugitives."

"Where is the von Salmuth-Tresckow lady now?" said Ursula. She gave a long shiver, and took a deep restorative breath, and let it out in an audible moan.

"She's clearing up matters at her house. She doesn't expect ever to see it again."

"She won't ever see it again," Edda put in. "Some roly-poly Russian general will install himself in there, along with half a dozen Soviet women soldiers, and it will take another war to get him out."

Ursula reached and ran a finger along her hairline, and turned to her daughter. "Sweetheart," she said, "will you help me pack our things?"

Within a moment, however, all three adults had turned and were regarding the girl, because Ingeborg gave no sign of moving. She stood motionless against the lighted rectangle of the demolished window, her hands at her side, the top of her head shining in the morning light. If her stomach was going round and round inside, as indeed it was, the others would not have known, as she looked collected, resolute, even, perhaps, a little accusatory. Moreover, when she gave out with her rehearsed proclamation, no one doubted the seriousness of what she had just said. She was staring at her mother. Her face shone like milk glass. "I'm not leaving here, Mommy," she said.

The strength of Ingeborg's character was known to all. It was Edda Holtzman who reacted first. "You don't know what you're saying," she said.

Otto explained the situation to Ingeborg in adult terms. "Ingeborg," he said, "there are Russian armies coming north and south of Berlin. You can hear them. Listen! In a day or two, they are going to meet right here and enclose Berlin. You'll be sealed off. You have no choice," he added.

"I am not going away," said Ingeborg.

"What about General Wenck?" said Ursula, grasping at straws. "They said on the radio he was fighting his way north and would relieve Berlin at any hour."

Otto gave visible signs of wonderment over Ursula's credulousness; he rubbed at his mustache with his knuckles. "What you heard on the radio, Utsie, was the radio. There is no reality in what you heard. You heard the *radio*."

"I wonder where our infallible leader is hiding during all these triumphs," Edda remarked tartly on the whereabouts of Hitler.

As always, Ursula reacted to Edda's seditious remarks with discomfort. "Aren't things bitter enough?"

Suddenly, with no advance sign whatever, Ingeborg made a hacking sound in her throat, her head jerked downward, and she started to vomit. There was not much of anything in her stomach to expel; what there was came down from her lips in a long lemon-colored drool. The nervous tensions of the past days, since the night of the horrific bombing, had gotten the best of her.

Ursula brought her a cup of water from the pail, while Andreas and the Holtzmans looked on with grave concern. Ingeborg refused the cup. She wiped her lips with her tongue. She had guessed her mother to be unequal, all this while, to the most important article of faith there ever was. Ingeborg would not pretend any longer to share her mother's despairing disbelief.

"I am waiting for Papa," she declared. She was eyeing Ursula levelly, and her announcement had in it something like the force of law. She didn't waver or blink. "He's alive, Mommy. He's coming home."

Edda blundered. "You can't know that," she said.

Ingeborg turned to Edda. "I do know," she said. "I am the only one who knows."

"But that's another matter," Otto put in.

"It is the only matter," Ingeborg came right back sharply. She wiped her mouth with the back of her fist.

"Your safety, Ingeborg," he said, "is a separate consideration altogether."

"I'm not in danger. I am not lost," she pointed out. "It is my father who is lost."

Ursula began to cry hearing that, and sat down on the bed with her coat on. Ingeborg was not crying. She stood stock-still, skinny as a wraith in the daylight. Her eyes challenged Otto to question her further. Otto saw the importance in doing just that.

"What would be the sense," he said, "if something terrible happened to you, and then he came home?"

"If I wait for him, nothing will happen to me."

"Ingeborg, you're not being reasonable," said Edda.

"Reasonable?" Ingeborg was a match for that line of argument. "Nothing is reasonable." Probably for the first time in her life ever, Ingeborg now put her precocious gifts on full display. She saw those around her as requiring of moral tuition. The words came to her lips unbidden. "Was it reasonable for everyone to leave me? Was it reasonable for

Herr Geissler to be burned to death in the schoolyard? Was it reasonable for Fräulein Falke to be crushed under a piano? Our house is smashed. Andreas is hungry every day. People are running away in the streets. I will *never* leave here!"

The Holtzmans and Ursula watched and listened in stunned silence.

"Until Papa returns," said Ingeborg. "Herr Haberzettl is staying, and I am staying. Betka," she said, "went away. She gave me her makeup kit, and went away. You go, Mommy. You take Andreas, and go. Because," she said, "I will never, never, never leave here."

Edda looked shocked. "Ingeborg!" she protested.

"Until," said Ingeborg, "my father comes back."

"You will have to take her by force," said Edda.

It was not possible for anyone present to read Ingeborg's thoughts, but she repeated Edda's word with a passion verging on contempt. *"Force?"*

"We're not like that," Ursula conceded, turning to her friend Edda. Ursula's nature shone through her words. "We don't force each other to do things."

"Your life and the lives of your two children may be in the balance," said Otto, austerely.

"They've been in the balance for a long time," said Ursula. "They were in the balance the night of the fourteenth. Look outdoors. Look at my home."

"Goebbels and his ministry have been right about one thing all these years," said Edda. "These Russians are sub-human."

Ursula sat listlessly on the edge of the bed, her shoulders slumped. "I don't believe that," she said.

"You'll come to believe it," said Otto, "if you stay here."

Ursula shook her head. "No, I have never believed that," she said.

Otto turned to Ingeborg and attempted a clever tack. "Ingeborg," he said, "you should be trying to convince your mother of the wisdom of her leaving here today. If she stays —"

Ingeborg saw through the ruse, and interrupted him in cold tones. "I am not leaving," she stated.

She stood in the window light like a skinny pillar of defiance, of moral steadfastness, in the midst of a growing chaos. Ingeborg had no wish to pain her mother, but could not restrain herself from stating certain facts that were supposed to have been withheld from her. She pointed a long, frail arm at the chest of drawers. "I know about the letters that came back from the front, Mommy. And I know what the army man told you on the telephone." Ingeborg waited for a reaction of the others to that, before concluding her thought. She was unbending. "He is alive," she said.

Once more, Edda made as though to object to Ingeborg's stubbornness and childish reasoning, but Ursula silenced her with a gesture.

"If I go away," said Ingeborg, "we'll never see him again. He'll be lost forever." From the nervous tension, as well perhaps as her undernourished condition, Ingeborg did in fact feel light-headed. But the thoughts she was expressing were convictions of long standing. She was positive in her heart, in her innocence, that if she retreated from this place, she would lose her faith; and if she lost that, he would not ever find his way back from wherever he was. "My waiting will bring him home."

Ursula's suppressed grief over the loss of Walter showed

in her face, and she put her fist to her forehead. Andreas
looked on in bewilderment, his eyes going worriedly from
his mother to his sister. Otto appeared openly disheartened
by what he was hearing. Hour by hour, the corridor to the
west was closing. It was common knowledge that the American front lines were opening up along the Elbe and that
German soldiers and civilians were pouring through to
safety in great numbers.

Ursula looked up at her daughter from where she was sitting. "You do want to stay, then," she confided.

Ingeborg felt no need to reply speedily or with emotion. "I
am not leaving here," she said.

Otto sighed aloud. He looked five years older than when
he had come into the room. "We'll wait downstairs for fifteen minutes," he said. "If you don't join us, we'll leave.
Another thing." Otto came back from the doorway. "Go
through all of your things, Ursula, and eliminate anything
and everything that is political. Nazi literature, books, magazines, pictures of Hitler, even picture postcards. Destroy
any and every sign of National Socialism."

Ursula, who had not risen from Ingeborg's bed, found it
odd that the enemy would be surprised upon finding Germans in Germany. She said as much.

"You have a naive side to you," said Otto, "that could
cost you your life. Half of these Russian soldiers come from
families that are all dead. Believe me, they are in a killing
frame of mind. For you," he said, "the war is no longer a radio news report. Within seventy-two hours, it will be coming up the stairs."

In a surprising response, Ursula reached with her arms for
Andreas. "We'll be all right," she said.

❖

For an hour, nonetheless, Ingeborg and Ursula paid heed to Otto Holtzman's parting admonitions, and went through all their belongings searching for any sign of the Nazi regime. Ingeborg was thinking all the while about Herr Welt, and told Ursula what she had seen there. "His front parlor looks like a *church*, Mommy. He's got little swastika flags everywhere, and a big picture of the Führer, and even some red and black draperies in the doorway to the next room."

"He is a party man," said Ursula. "If anyone knows what to do, I'm certain he does."

Here Ingeborg's appreciation of the block warden's possible want of astuteness came out. "I don't think he does, Mommy."

"What is more," said Ursula, reluctantly, "people like Herr Welt will be scattering in all directions. Like that S.S. man you saw changing clothes downstairs."

Abruptly, Ursula's maternal instincts prompted her to take hold of her two children and give them some courage. She doubtless suspected that Ingeborg's adamant resolution to stay was quite a separate thing from the deep fears she must surely be experiencing in the face of what was coming. She clasped the two of them. "We're going to be all right," she said. "I'll keep you safe. In a few days, the war will be over. We'll fix up our house, and you'll both go back to school."

Ingeborg was staring point-blank at her mother's face. Usually undemonstrative, Ingeborg kissed her mother and leaned her head against her. It was just what she had wanted to hear.

"I'll get gifts for both of you, and make nice warm suppers." Ursula spoke in low tones.

"And," Ingeborg prompted her, "we'll go back to school."

"Yes, you will."

Shortly before noon, an entire German infantry regiment, moving down from the northern front to the southern, passed directly through Potsdam. Most were on foot. They came in an hour-long column down Spandauerstrasse and into Ingeborg's own street. A narrow way had been cleared through the rubble of Charlottenstrasse. The soldiers were noticeably haggard. Their uniforms were rumpled and dirty. There was much plaster dust in the air. Men of a second detachment coming over the river from a supply depot by the train station had to overturn some of the dozens of wrecked civilian vehicles near the ruins of the town palace to get through with their supply trucks. Ingeborg watched from the window as they passed below in the street. Many were without helmets or field packs. Whenever an airplane sounded, they all looked up. The column curled around the two derelict trolley cars in a dusty, gray-green stream, and passed along with a constant shuffling sound. Toward the end of the column came an open civilian truck. Ingeborg could see down into it. There were seven or eight nurses in back. They were all lying asleep on the bed of the truck. After that, came an ambulance, an open staff car, and four horse-pulled wagons. After the last wagon went by, a silence developed. The sun came and went on the cobbled street.

That afternoon, Ingeborg went round the corner to Herr Welt's door on Jägerstrasse. She was quite sure he was not at home, as he was a member of the Volksturm, which was made up mostly of boys and elderly men, and which was quite active lately. Ingeborg was mistaken. After knocking twice, the door opened for her. It was Werner Welt. He looked tired and distracted; he looked downhearted. She suspected that he had been sitting indoors, doing nothing, probably for a long while. Or maybe he had been looking at the big gardening book that lay open on the table behind him. In either case, within minutes, Ingeborg was collecting all of his National Socialist paraphernalia, and was stuffing anything that would burn into the cast-iron stove. Of all the people Ingeborg had known, she believed that Otto Holtz-man was the most reliable authority. She felt certain he was right about eliminating Nazi symbols, books, pictures, and such. As for Herr Welt, he was noticeably helpless, looking both pliant and listless. Ingeborg took over.

"Werner," she said, going to the stove, "I need a match."

Having undergone so much emotional stress that morn-ing, concerning Otto and Edda's departure for Lübeck, it re-laxed her to be able to be a little bossy. While the thought may never have occurred to her before, Ingeborg knew in her heart that she had become the most important and best-loved person in Werner Welt's life. She didn't think about it; she just acted it out. "You stir the fire with the poker," she said. "Otherwise, the books will not burn up."

She was addressing him in polite but assertive accents. She was like the lady of superior blood, who, in the pages of an exciting romance, had arrived out of nowhere, in the nick of time, to protect the life and well-being of a devoted serv-ing man. She was one of her own romantic heroines, who was never wanting in courage or foresight, and who never forgot that persons in lower stations were not unworthy of special care.

Before long, Ingeborg took the poker from Werner. "I'll stir the fire. You take the pictures down." She had stuffed the long red and black draperies in through the lid opening, and worked the poker busily in the fire. She put in piles of

Nazi circulars, magazines, envelopes containing directives, and a stack of party newspapers. She worked at it for many minutes. The sides of the stove glowed a cherry color.

As matters progressed, and more and more of Werner's party artifacts found their way into the stove, Werner Welt asked her advice. He asked her twice about the World War I picture of his unit.

"Leave that one up, Werner. I already told you. Take down the picture of the Führer."

The block warden's dilemma, and much of the cause of his psychical maladies on this day, found a focus in the portrait of Adolf Hitler. He removed it from the wall. It was big. He held it in both hands.

"Where should I put it?"

"You're not going to put it anywhere, Werner."

Ingeborg stood at the stove, with the long silky blond tail of her hair reaching down her back, her face glowing ruddily from the grate of the fire. The room was hot. She had taken off her coat and was wearing an old, faded, rather frilly blue-and-purple-striped dress that accentuated her bony arms and legs. Werner Welt was perspiring from the heat. His spectacles were fogged. Had their circumstance been transposed backward in time to the Middle Ages, and far away to some Middle Eastern outpost threatened by Islam, with the picture in hand being that of the Holy Savior himself, Ingeborg's next injunction would not have differed in the slightest. "You're going to smash it," she said.

"I couldn't do that," he replied.

"There would be no sense in burning all of those flags and things if you are not going to destroy that." Her reasoning was unassailable, and her pinched lips and bright eyes reinforced it.

"There are some things, Fräulein Maas, that you don't understand."

As earlier in the day, Ingeborg gave somebody a taste of her advanced intellect.

"There are many things I don't understand," she instructed, "but what is going to happen to that picture is not one of them." Her eyes widened imperatively.

She enjoyed looking at him in this way, where they both knew that her decision was final.

"I can't do it, Fräulein."

Ingeborg set the poker across the top of the stove, took the big framed picture from him, and set it down on the floor at an angle against the stove. Then she took hold of the poker.

"You won't do this for me?" she said, hoping in her secret heart that he would *not* be able to. For Ingeborg, the picture of the Führer was understandably a very solemn thing, as she had been indoctrinated all her life to understand. But in her own egotistical, childish mind, she was about to demonstrate to her "gardener," once and for all, whom he would be looking up to in future, as she raised the long, smoke-blackened poker in both hands and commenced to swing it with astonishing vigor. Nor was there any subconscious drag that might have caused her to strike at the edges of the picture glass. The first blow hit the Führer dead center. The glass exploded. Herr Welt looked on with a gaping and startled expression on his sweated face, as the delicate-limbed Ingeborg hit the picture again and again, twenty or thirty times. Each blow gave back a report like the crack of a gunshot, as she reduced the picture and the frame surrounding it to bits of rubbish.

If Ingeborg had an inner strength that others might lack, and if that characteristic had been pressed to its limits that morning, the display that she put on with the poker for the benefit of her admiring neighbor was perhaps an understandable purgation. She stood by the stove with panting breast as Werner knelt and gathered up the bits of glass and shattered wood. While she was at it, Ingeborg had a half mind to smash the picture on the piano of the young woman named Stephanie, Werner's ancient heartthrob. Ingeborg thought her smug and coarse-looking, and wondered how her friend could have suffered the sight of her on the piano all these years.

For the better part of an hour, Ingeborg kept the blaze going in the stove, adding whole drawerfuls of Nazi pamphlets, handbooks, even some personal commendations. In the meanwhile, Werner's spirits improved. He made coffee for them.

"No one has ever helped me before," he said, innocently, without self-pity, while bearing teacups to the table.

Ingeborg's response was automatic. "You never made a garden for anyone before."

"This week," the warden confessed, "that is all I have been thinking about."

"Have you been going to your job?" she asked.

Herr Welt said nothing.

"Have you been eating?" she asked.

"I don't remember eating. I have coffee to drink. I don't really want any food."

Ingeborg replaced the lid on the stove while watching him. He was setting out her teacup with great care, as if it were the most precious piece of Meissen china ever manufactured. Ingeborg guessed shrewdly that Werner Welt had enjoyed no private life whatever for a long time, except for his minor post with the party, and was dejected to the point of paralysis by the impending collapse.

Herr Welt held Ingeborg's chair for her when she came to the table to sit. Ingeborg enjoyed the solicitude. The block warden's house had become for her like a theater, a sanctuary in which her romantic egoism was given scope for development. "Werner," she said, "your house is very dark and dusty. I'm going to help you decorate it." She spoke these words while making a pretense of examining a page of hollyhocks in the big gardening book. Werner could not help laughing. He loved Ingeborg and saw through her histrionic airs to the vain creature inside. Ingeborg cut short his amusement.

"Another thing," she said, "I can't stand looking at that picture."

"Stephanie?" Werner was genuinely startled by her criticism and the speed of her retort. "Why?"

"Because it's ugly," she said.

Werner was gaping then through his thick spectacles at the picture on the piano. "Stephanie?" he said again.

"Werner," Ingeborg disabused him in blunt terms, "she is a very ugly woman. Her nose is too big, she has fat on her neck, her lips stick out like a fish."

"That's not true." He shook his head incredulously.

"If you want to keep it," she said, "it shouldn't be in your parlor. Especially," Ingeborg added, with inspiration, "if you were ever to put a picture of me up in this room. Because I will not allow my picture to be shown in the same room with that."

By now, Ingeborg was able to anticipate her neighbor's reactions to her rapid locutions. The prospect of someday hanging a picture of Ingeborg in his parlor brought a winey color to his cheekbones. "I would like to put up your picture," he allowed, quietly. "I would enlarge it to a good size."

"I wouldn't mind if it were enormous," she said.

When the coffee was heated, Ingeborg shut the gardening book and sat back. It was not polite to be preoccupied when someone had prepared something for you and was desirous of your company. She wished also to dwell in her mind on the type of picture she would like put up in her honor and visualized a fur-trimmed cloak over her shoulders, a friendly but not intimate expression on her lips, and her long glowing hair falling dreamily into darkness. For Ingeborg, Herr Welt's apartment was a quiet and restful place in the heart of the shattered city; her imagination expanded. One day, she would call on her neighbor, and he would lead her outdoors to her big sunlit garden. Maybe Frau Redeker, her teacher, would join her on her white swing in the gazebo, and they would sit reading their favorite books, while Werner snipped and pruned. There would be no dog-fights in the sky. The earth would stop trembling. And when you went into the street, to go to school, or to buy sausage or apples, there would not be that eternal refugee sitting on the curb, on the bundle of his things, in despair, come to the end of his strength. There would be none of that, or of the constant, mind-breaking worry.

She was thinking once more about the dog show; her father in his eggshell jacket, coming to her at the picnic table that afternoon, carrying soft drinks and something for her to eat. She could picture it clearly. Dogs everywhere on leashes; an orange-and-white-striped tent; the straw in the soda bottle he set before her.

Within days, the important choices that one might have made, whether to stay or go, were foreclosed by events, as the so-called escape corridor to the west was sealed off by the encircling Soviet armies of Konev and Zhukov. For at least one day, an unexpected calm fell over the city. A light rain was falling, which probably accounted for the relative quiet in the skies. When Ursula went to her job at Wilhelm Platz, she found no one there, and came back home in the rain. From every direction came the rumble of artillery, a soft incessant thunder as of a spring storm that would neither relent nor pass, but which by now had become as much a part of the weather as the splash of raindrops on the windowsill. While a steamy smoke still sifted up from the foundations of collapsed buildings, and the streets lay strewn with rubble and stalled vehicles, virtually no one was outdoors. Ursula followed a serpentine path through the debris in the heart of Charlottenstrasse. Here and there, the trolley rails gleamed wetly. She recalled her first day in Potsdam, coming this very way on foot with her children; how she had marveled somewhat at the solidity and prosperous aspect of the streets, the businesses, the imperial edifices. It was once a famous and much-loved place, with its garrisons, palaces, archives, cathedral, and the big gracious hotels round the Old Market. Long ago, Frederick the Great had lived here in the summertime, like a hermit, with his dogs. Now, whole streets were gone. The linden tree by the corner pump was split in two, as though halved by the swing of a magnificent axe. Before turning in at her own door, Ursula was met by a peculiar sight. Three streets away, where Hohenzollernstrasse crossed her own street, a solitary black horse came clopping across amid the ruins, and continued without pausing, its head down, till it was out of sight.

At noontime, when the rain let up, Ursula made up her mind to take her two children to the park of the summer palace. She had taken it in her thoughts to spend what might well turn out to be their last such time together on earth in a peaceful and ordinary way; an hour in pleasant spring environs, among the trees and pathways of Sans Souci.

It was not a long walk to the park. It had stopped raining, but Ingeborg and Andreas were wearing the identical dark blue rain hats that had been given to Ursula as a birthday gift from Dr. Naumann's wife at the hospital several weeks ago. Along the way, from behind a stuccoed wall, came the clinking of a shovel; someone digging a pit to bury the family silver. Ursula was struck by the absurdity of someone hiding their valuables. Ursula had no valuables except for those two that she was leading through the street on either hand. She wished devotedly that she could hide the two of them away and collect them again on some sunshiny day. Unlike her daughter, Ursula Maas held out no hope for Walter. Like so many millions of others, the dear sweet boy that she had married one rainy Saturday in 1932, in a chapel of St. Hedwig's Cathedral, in Berlin, was gone forever. She would not see him again; not on this earth.

In the park, the three of them paused to rest and sit on a stone outcropping not far from the Oriental teahouse. Ursula smoked a cigarette; a habit she often indulged when physically tired from work, or as in years past when socializing, with a glass of brandy, in the evening. It was that kind of day. Except for the rolling thunder of the long-range pieces, the soft interlude expanded in time. The park, although pitted with bomb craters, and seared here and there with the blackened remains of refugee campfires, was turning green.

There were crocuses everywhere, trees in bud, even dandelions. When Ursula told Andreas that she could make them a very tasty salad from dandelions if he could find a sufficient number, Andreas responded with boyish pride and a burst of activity that set him darting about in every direction. Each time he returned with one of the young plants, Ursula made a show of putting it away safely in her bag. Ingeborg indulged her brother in her inimitable way.

"Andreas is better at finding things than anyone else," she said, and showed him a prim, endearing smile.

"Yes, he is," said Ursula. "I would not have found even one dandelion by now."

"Neither would I," chimed Ingeborg.

"While Andreas has found six."

Andreas was enlivened by the compliments. "I think I saw another one by that same tree," he piped, before departing like a shot.

Ingeborg sat on the boulder beside her mother. She had removed her rain hat. She appeared thoughtful for a long moment before speaking up. "Mommy, do you remember that soldier who talked to me at Herr Haberzettl's on Christmas Eve?"

Ursula remembered. "The boy who liked you?" she said, teasingly, recognizing at once Ingeborg's preadolescent crush.

One of the rarest sights ever in those days would have been that of Ingeborg blushing. Her temples reddened instantly, and her lips twisted as she gazed off sidewise with a caught look.

At the sight of Ingeborg discomfited, Ursula ran the flat of her hand lovingly over her glowing head. "I remember him very well," she said. "He was very handsome. Did you think he was?"

Ingeborg had turned and was avoiding her mother's eyes. "I suppose so," she said.

Ursula was gazing at the crown of Ingeborg's head. "What was his name, sweetheart?"

"Franzi."

"Yes, that was his name. I remember. You probably didn't notice," said Ursula, "but I think he liked you very much."

Ingeborg could not meet her mother's eyes. "I didn't notice," she said, evasively.

"I thought he was very taken with you."

"Did you?"

Ursula reached and toyed with a tress of Ingeborg's hair, running it through her fingers. She was touched by the sight of Ingeborg infatuated. It was the very first time that Ursula had ever seen her baby girl betray such feelings. "Did you want to write to him?" she asked.

"I wouldn't know how to," Ingeborg confessed, quietly. She looked up at her mother then for the first time. "I don't know his last name. But I know the name of his village. It's in Thuringia."

"What is the name?"

"He comes from a place called Hildsburghausen. He said it's very small."

"Then it should be easy," Ursula assured. "You just write on the envelope 'To Lt. Franzi, Unknown Last Name, Hildsburghausen.' I'm certain he'll get it. If you wanted," said Ursula, "you could write something on the back of the envelope to help the postman in Hildsburghausen. You could say, 'Franzi was at the Officers Training Barracks, Potsdam Garrison, in January 1945. He is about eighteen, of average height, with short blond hair, and is very handsome.' "

Ingeborg was visibly taken by the realistic prospect opening before her of re-establishing communication with an admirer who happened to be the handsomest soldier on earth.

"He would get it, Mommy?"

"You could also add, on the envelope," said Ursula, unable to resist the temptation to fire her daughter's vanity, " 'I am Ingeborg, his girlfriend.' "

Ingeborg jumped. She couldn't believe her ears. *That would be horrible!*

Ursula seized hold of her and was squeezing her. "My little heartbreaker."

Ingeborg remained scandalized. "I would never write that! That would be so improper. . . . Besides, he's in the army. He's not at Hildsburghausen."

Ursula reassured her on that point. "He will be there soon enough," she said. "He'll be home very soon."

"Because the war is ending?"

"Just about."

"Will the post office be open again?"

"Yes, it will."

Ingeborg's thoughts remained on track during the ensuing silence. She spoke from curiosity. "Franzi is a farmer, Mommy. Did you know that?"

"I didn't."

"Is that a good thing to be? Could someone be a farmer and a bookseller?"

Ursula sustained the fanciful conversation. "Well," she replied, "a lady could be a bookseller, and her husband could be a farmer."

Ursula kept an eye out for Andreas's whereabouts. For the moment, he was out of sight. Several armored cars went past on a road west of the park. They could be seen beyond the trees.

Sensing Ingeborg staring at her, Ursula turned to her instinctively. "What is it?" She thought she had never seen such a concentrated, passionate look on her daughter's face. It took her unawares.

Ingeborg replied subduedly: "If you and I were ever separated — I would wait for you."

Instantly, Ursula felt the heat rising to her eyes.

"If I know nothing else," said Ursula, "I know that to be true."

They both watched Andreas running toward them from the direction of the flowering almond by the teahouse. Ingeborg completed her thought.

"I would wait forever," she said.

On the way home, Ingeborg caught a glimpse of something quite startling, if only because, given the desperate condition of everyone's lives, it was so remarkably ordinary. Through an open window, at the corner of Lindenstrasse, a girl in a white blouse and black skirt was tap dancing. The staccato rhythm of her tapping shoes on the wooden floor echoed in the street. She was dancing to the strains of a light air that someone (out of sight) was plinking out for her on a piano. Ingeborg recognized her. It was the Hitler Youth girl who was standing behind her that day in the queue at the food shop, and who had reviled somebody from the back of the line for their defeatist remarks. She had lost three brothers in the war, she said. But seeing her dancing now, Ingeborg knew better who she was. She was enrolled in the upper forms at school, a student tap dancer who performed in school stage productions. Hansi Heiss had mentioned her once or twice. Her name was Olivia Jupp. Hansi said that his brother, Bübchen, called her Olivia Jupp Jupp, and did hilarious impersonations of Olivia's tap dancing which produced shrieks of laughter by all of those lucky enough to be present. Hansi had shown Ingeborg and the others the look of idiotic concentration that Bübchen created on his face during his moments of inspired buffoonery, while dancing up and down in army boots.

For three or four minutes, Ingeborg and her mother and brother remained standing in the street, watching and listening. To a third party, to another observer, the sight of Ursula Maas and her two children, with their shiny rain hats, standing motionless amid the debris, gazing up at a gaping window, might have seemed as unworldly and jarring to the senses as the sight of the dancing girl inside.

Despite Bübchen's frolicsome parody of the girl, and the fact that she had frightened Ingeborg that day in the food shop queue, Ingeborg couldn't help admiring her. She liked her looks and probably saw the dark-haired, tap-dancing Olivia Jupp as a desirable friend to take Betka's place. She liked the fact, also, that Olivia, for whatever the cause or reason, had not run away.

Presently, the girl inside spotted the three of them watching her from the street and came at once to close off the window. Ingeborg wanted to speak to her. She was getting used to being noticed, and removed her shiny blue rain hat that the Jupp girl might see her more clearly. But Ursula, who appeared charmed by the girl's dance, or maybe by the bizarre quality of the moment, or maybe even by something ongoing and hopeful in it, spoke up first.

"That was delightful to watch," she said.

"Thank you." Olivia Jupp offered Ingeborg's mother a thin, wary smile, while reaching left and right for the curtains.

To her own surprise, Ingeborg spoke out impulsively. "You dance beautifully, Olivia!"

The girl in the white blouse hesitated momentarily, her arms stretched out, then nodded decorously to Ingeborg and flashed her an affectionate smile. A second later, the curtains shot to before her with dramatic finality, as of the sudden closing to view of an entire age.

The makeshift clinic was once a customs warehouse. It had a big central elevator operated by pulleys and an old hydraulic system. No one used that anymore. The upper floor of the building housed trauma cases. Some of the patients were off their heads. The worst cases were taken away. One of the soldiers insisted on speaking Italian, even though his Italian was very bad and painful to listen to. Another soldier sat by his cot at the far end of the room and gazed out over the rooftops to the dark waters of the Baltic. He stared outdoors by the hour, as at a movie screen that no one else could see. Sissi, a local farm girl who helped out, often packed and lit the man's pipe for him. She had a soft spot for him. She thought him sad.

Somebody had brought a coal lighter into the harbor. They were going to try, they said, to move the last dozen or so soldiers west to safety. The Russians were getting close. Someone told Sissi that the Russians were nailing women to barn doors. The day the men were evacuated, Sissi was the last person to leave the building. She saw them all off to the harbor, then walked in deep thought all the way back through town, and out the gravel road under the oak trees, past the tanner's house and the creamery, toward home.

4

THE FINAL BLOW fell not forty-eight hours later, coming in the form of a long, shambling, ragtag column of Russian troops pushing their way noisily into the northern suburbs. They came swarming. Pressing forward among them, and reaching back for two miles, were trucks, farm wagons, horse-drawn fieldpieces, battered German cars, motorcycles, even mounted fur-hatted cossacks. This first column was crude and disorganized. Two or three dozen infantrymen were sitting atop two buses packed full of liberated Russian women and children, the soldiers on top firing their rifles in the air and giving throaty outcries. *"Uri! Uri! Hitler kaputt!"* Draped over the sides of trucks were Persian rugs, sacks of household goods, clothing, even musical instruments. The mood was boisterous. An exuberant crackle of rifle fire was constant. Toward the rear of the column were a dozen horse-drawn supply wagons, and following them two or three American-made trucks carrying some of the wounded watched over by uniformed nurses armed with machine pistols. The picture of an ancient Eastern warrior band on the move was completed by the sight of cattle moving along in the grass athwart the column, and, last of all, a big hay wagon.

Not a mile away, however, clanking in noisily along an adjacent roadway, came a string of massive T-34 tanks, the commanders in black helmets standing up in their open hatches, the treads chewing up cobbles and tar. Dusty staff cars carrying regimental officers, intelligence personnel, and Soviet political agents were squeezed in among the trundling tanks. Red flags were draped over many tanks and trucks. An enormous photo of Joseph Stalin was affixed to the tailgate of a two-and-a-half-ton Studebaker. Loot was in evidence all along the line, especially Oriental carpets dangling from the backs of tanks. Riflemen rode atop. Now and again, a motorcyclist slid forward through the armored column with map instructions for the lead tanks.

There was no opposition. The shattered remains of the German Ninth Army under General Busse, and its so-called ambulating *"Kessel,"* containing thousands of German civilian refugees, had connected with General Wenck's Twentieth Army in the vicinity of Ferch, south of Potsdam, and both were withdrawing toward the Elbe in hasty disarray. Berlin was sealed off, and would fall in a matter of days, or even hours.

The night before, Ursula had taken what measures she could in order to protect her children and herself from the coming calamity. She was quite certain all along that the first two or three days would be critical, a time of savagery, plundering, shootings, and rape. If she could conceal the two of them and herself during that lawless interval, they might survive the end of it. Ingeborg was impressed by her mother's outward calmness and foresight that evening, as Ursula prepared to take them across the way to the cellar of the rectory. Cellars were not especially safe places, Ursula explained to Ingeborg, not from marauding soldiers, but because the rectory was an empty house, from top to bottom, to looting soldiers it would seem a less likely hiding place for civilians. Ursula had found a crucifix in the front hall of the rectory, which she nailed to the front door. "To discourage wickedness," she said. At this moment, she actually smiled at Ingeborg, who, by now, could not conceal her fright; she followed at her mother's heels wherever she went. She was very proud of her mother, and was very taken once again at how resourceful, courageous, and beautiful she was. Ingeborg felt helpless. Once or twice, she wished that her mother had taken Andreas, and gone away with Otto and Edda, and left her behind to keep vigil for her father, because Ingeborg, for all her innocence, knew that her mother was in the greatest danger of all. Ingeborg knew the word "rape," and knew it to signify something both mysterious and frightening, while unable to form pictures in her mind of what exactly it meant. She had an icy apprehension of enemy soldiers doing horrible things to her mother, even perhaps finally killing her.

"You should have left with Otto and Edda," she said at one point.

"I, alone?" said Ursula.

"You and Andreas," said Ingeborg.

"Andreas and I, without you?"

"Yes," said Ingeborg.

Ursula was not unaware that Ingeborg was following her step by step everywhere she went. She ran a hand over her daughter's head. "The world isn't made that way, and your mother isn't made that way. Besides — I'm glad we stayed."

"*You are?*" Ingeborg exclaimed, with a note of desperation.

"Yes. Otherwise," Ursula said, "I would never have known how wonderfully you are made."

Ingeborg gaped at her mother with her mouth open. "Say it again," she said.

"I'm glad we stayed, Ingeborg."

Later, in the cellar of the rectory, Ursula moved the cot into the coal room behind the slatted partition; then all three returned across the street to get the few food provisions that Ursula had managed to find and save. She had cold tea, an opened can of corned beef, some biscuits, and probably best of all, eight hard-boiled eggs. She brought her flashlight, candles, Andreas's box of chess pieces, and, of all things, for herself, an American fashion magazine that Edda had found someplace. Nor was Ursula finished with her preparations to hide her children. To give the basement a more derelict look, she removed the boards from the broken cellar windows, overturned the table, and left the blown-in rear cellar door by the stairs. The following afternoon, when the first crackle of rifle fire reached their ears, she took the two wicker chairs upstairs, and threw them out the front door. She left the door wide.

Ingeborg asked why she had thrown the chairs down the front steps.

"It will look," said Ursula, "as though the house has already been entered and ransacked, and that no one would be apt to be left hiding indoors. We'll be all right in a day or two," she said.

"And then," said Andreas, uncertain of his meanings, "will the war be over?"

"Yes."

By nightfall, however, Ursula's own apparent calm began to unravel. To begin with, some armed opposition did develop in the suburb of Brandenburger, out by the park, and there was a brief but explosive exchange of tank fire and panzerfausts not a hundred yards from the Langen Bridge. The resistance was sporadic. By late evening, Russian soldiery was pouring into the streets. Sitting in the dark, hour after hour, and listening to the ongoing noise of the foot traffic and motorcycles in the streets, the shouts, the impulsive rifle fire, even the singing, or sudden blare of accordions and brass instruments, was unnerving. Unknown to Ursula, hours earlier the Hamburg radio station had broadcast an announcement of the death of Hitler in Berlin. Grand Admiral Karl Doenitz, who had succeeded to the chancellorship, later addressed the prostrate nation from the city of Plön. It was Ingeborg who guessed at the truth. She whispered to her mother. "They keep saying, *'Hitler kaputt!'* He must be dead."

Ursula and Ingeborg sat on the cot, wrapped in a blanket, their backs to the wall of the basement. Andreas was sleeping fitfully. Before withdrawing into the coal room, Ursula had piled several lengths of lumber against the slatted partition to help conceal the enclosure, and had managed with difficulty to pull an old wood box up close to the door. From time to time, through the long cracks in the partition, came the filtered glare of passing headlights shining into the cellar. The night was nerve-racking. Ingeborg might have been less fearful then, but time and again felt the spasmodic quaking of her mother's body. As dawn developed, casting a soft gray light into the tiny room, Ingeborg saw her mother's lips moving in prayer. Ursula looked hypnotized.

Outdoors, the brawling and drunken revelry grew. The throaty alien language of the soldiers, discerned amid the clatter of hooves and wheels, was fearsome in itself. Shouts of *"Uri! Uri! Frau! Frau!"* and the gunshots and laughter intensified. At one point, a woman's earsplitting scream penetrated the walls of the house, followed by a sound of breaking glass and a second scream from the woman. There followed the thud of running footsteps, a male shout close by, the smashing sound of a bottle bursting, and a third scream. Ursula was rocking to and fro. She couldn't restrain herself. "It's getting very bad," she said, her voice thin and uneven.

"You're shaking, Mommy," said Andreas.

Indeed, Ursula was losing control of her wits; she looked to be verging on shock. She repeated herself many times. "It's getting worse!" She said it over and over. She was clasping and unclasping her hands. "Please God, dear God, my children, my children —!"

The upstairs front door burst in against the foyer wall with a crash that shook the rectory. There were heavy footsteps overhead. A woman, being dragged in, was screaming. There was much gruff shouting and more drumming footsteps. A gunshot went off upstairs — it was the blunt bang of a revolver — and then an explosion of glass. The woman was pleading. Suddenly, one of the Russian soldiers shouted at the woman in German, *"I'm no angel!"* He said more, but his words were drowned out by a piping harmonica and the heavy thumping rhythms of a soldier dancing noisily on the floorboards of the front room. *"Voyna kaputt!"* Two more pistol shots sounded. Then an argument erupted, with one Russian soldier shouting at another, while from the front of the house the dancing footsteps continued without letup. From time to time, came the perceptible echo of soldiers climbing the stairs to the upper stories and coming down again. The voice of the woman sounded occasionally overhead, from the room directly above the coal room, where, it could be guessed, she was being raped repeatedly.

One man came downstairs into the cellar. Ingeborg could make him out between the slats of the partition. He was talking or humming to himself, and stepped out the gaping doorway into the yard. She could tell he was not a big man. He wore lace-up boots that did not match his uniform. The laces were untied. He was hatless. He stood taking deep breaths of the morning air. His face was flushed very red, from alcohol. Presently, something odd transpired. The man was talking to someone. A dog appeared to view in the yard, by the door. Ingeborg recognized the animal. She had seen him more than once by the Kanal. He was a big black dog. He looked very starved. The soldier was talking to him. He was having a conversation with the dog. It sounded like a very reasonable and thoughtful conversation. It sounded musical; and all the while the drunken soldier spoke, the crazed dog gaped at him with its head extended and its tail down. The man seemed to be philosophizing. Then he took out a chunk of bread and gave half to the dog. The dog ate it hungrily. The man then had something more to say, something clearly also reasonable, like one wayfarer remarking to another upon some profound point of interest in his travels. The soldier breathed deeply again, then gave the dog the remainder of the bread. As the soldier came back indoors, reeling slightly, he climbed the stairs and continued to talk over his shoulder to the dog in the same philosophical vein. The big dog followed him up the stairs, his tail going.

By midday, despite the continuing noise and bustle of men and horses and vehicles in the street, the rectory had grown quiet. Ingeborg had shown herself in this last day or two to be possessed of a special quality of moral or spiritual endurance, as at this time when she reached and opened the traveling bag in which her mother had packed their food, and began slicing biscuits in two, and tapping the shells of hard-boiled eggs. If it was not evident till now, although it had been many times before, Ingeborg Maas had reserves of strength that went beyond clinical citation. Two or three times that morning, during the mayhem, when the violence upstairs was mounting to a pitch, she had felt an impulse to open the door and go upstairs and put a stop to it. She understood her mother's fears but did not suffer them to a notable extent. Quite a long while ago, back in the weeks of this autumn and winter, in the desperate hours of her having had to conquer dread after dread over the fate of her father, she had learned to suppress fear. At this moment, somewhere in the world, her father was sitting just as she was, leaned forward with a spoon in his hand, tapping the shell of a hard-boiled egg. While her world was no bigger than the street she lived on, it was not smaller than her colossal heart. Wherever he was, the spring sun was shining. The almond trees were in flower.

S till, in the days to come, Ingeborg and Andreas were never more than a step away from their mother. The war, it was announced, was officially ended. With the arrival in Potsdam of a Soviet military police battalion, the city was promptly made secure against the random violence of soldiers in the street, even though no effort was made to feed the civilian population. The search for something to eat became for all a full-time occupation. Ingeborg was with her mother in the Old Market one afternoon when some Volksturm boys came home from Babelsberg across the river;

they had been released by their Russian captors and told to go home. They came hurrying, half running, over the Langen Bridge, eight or nine of them, all in uniform. Dietmar Kohl, a fourteen-year-old from Herr Geissler's class, was one of them. It was clear he had been living in terror for days. Ingeborg recognized him. As he ran past, his face under the peak of his forage cap told it all. He looked drained and sweated. He was running home to his mother.

By an irony, the rectory across the street from Ingeborg's house was set up as staff headquarters by a Russian intelligence officer. The sight of the big red flag at the door, and the presence of a twenty-four-hour sentry, soon seemed as ordinary as the general spectacle of the streets crowded with displaced Germans and Slavic soldiers. The Russian colonel possessed the mundane police records of everyone in the neighborhood, and all day long inhabitants were summoned, questioned, and sent home. The efficiency of the Soviet occupiers came as a surprise to the citizenry. Ursula Maas was herself questioned one day by a Soviet captain on the intelligence staff. The interview took place in the downstairs front parlor of the rectory. Before speaking, the captain leafed through a very long list of names of known Nazis and sympathizers. He was a biggish man with a pocked complexion. The interrogation was brief. Following each reply she gave, the Russian officer nodded, muttering something in Russian that sounded to Ursula like "Tak, tak," and set her reply to paper.

"Your children are ten years old and six."

Ursula sat on a wooden chair in front of his table. "Yes."

"Your husband?" he said.

"Is dead," said Ursula.

The Russian officer glanced up expressionlessly, made a

throat-clearing sound, then straightened the papers on the table before him, and made a careful entry with his pencil.

The captain had a disarming manner of phrasing questions in a melodic, offhand way. He continued writing while speaking. "Are you a National Socialist?" he asked, amiably.

"No," Ursula began to reply, "I —"

"Why?" he asked, and looked up.

Ursula hesitated. "I am not political," she said. She was sitting forward on her chair, her hands on her lap.

He smiled cynically. "You were *opposed?*" he said.

"No," Ursula admitted, "I was not opposed to the Nazi party or our government. But I have no party number or card." She didn't know what else to say. She was visibly anxious. Through the window facing the street and walkway, she could see the blond crown of Ingeborg's head. Her daughter was waiting for her by the steps. The intelligence officer had not looked up from his records or form.

"Your husband was killed?" he said.

"Yes," Ursula replied.

"When was he killed?" The captain was writing. He paused to touch the pencil point to his tongue.

"Last summer," she replied, faintly.

"Was he a party member?" Again, the question was put amiably.

"No, he was not."

"Are you sure of that?"

"Yes. I am certain of it."

As before, the Russian looked up at her with a wry expression. "Was he opposed to Hitler and that government?"

Ursula was sure the officer would not believe her and couldn't bring herself to reply. "Yes," she said, at last, truthfully, "he was."

The Russian nodded in belief, satisfied that the manner of his questions had produced a truthful response. *"Tak, tak,"* he said, with a genial smile, and wrote something down. "If you change address," he added, "you must come here and tell us."

"Is that all?" said Ursula.

"Have you heard of Oranienburg?" he asked.

"Yes," said Ursula, "this week."

"And Sachsenhausen?"

"I have heard about the camps, yes." Ursula glanced up at the ceiling anxiously, then away to the window again. For a week, since the announcement of the end of the war, there was talk in the streets of nothing but the concentration camps. Sometimes her eyes filled with tears.

The captain took a small white card from the tabletop, wrote something in Cyrillic upon it, the word "Interrogated" in German, set down the date, "14 May 1945," and signed his name, "Capt. Boris Malyushenka." He extended it to Ursula. "If you are summoned by someone else to be interrogated, show them that."

"Thank you," said Ursula.

"Tomorrow," the Russian continued, as he put away the form he had filled out, "many of you will be going by truck and bus to visit Oranienburg for the afternoon."

Ursula had heard one eyewitness account already by a civilian refugee from the north who had been forced to visit Sachsenhausen, and look there upon the living dead of the inmates. "Please don't make me go," she said.

"I do not decide these things."

"Please," she said.

The Russian opened his hands to signify his inability to affect such steps.

"I haven't the strength," said Ursula. "I'm not like that." She didn't know what else to say. She felt the tears welling and strove to fight them off.

The officer was looking at her in a placid, not hostile way, and nodded understandingly. *"Tak, tak,"* he said.

While going out the door, with her head bowed, Ursula met a Russian woman coming in. The woman was of impressive size and was wearing an army uniform with red shoulder tabs and a leather-billed service hat. As they met in the open doorway, the woman reached and put her hands flat to Ursula's chest, and with a curse thrust Ursula violently backward against the hallway wall out of her way. Ingeborg saw it happen; she saw the look of shock and the cowed expression on her mother's face, as she collected herself and came out the door. Despite all the hardship, she had never seen her mother suffer such an indignity. To Ingeborg, her mother was inviolate, like one of the oil depictions at church of the holiest of women. Some transgressions were unthinkable. Ingeborg stood on the walkway, with her mouth open and her fist to her forehead, gaping at Ursula as she came out to join her. Back home, in their room above the Falke apartment (which had been thoroughly plundered of its furnishings, carpets, embroidered pillows), Ingeborg washed her mother's hair. She had never done that before, but she insisted. She warmed water in a pan on the electric heater. Ursula understood, and allowed herself to be spoiled; she enjoyed the loving treatment. "You're more than a mother deserved."

Day by day, the entire district was sinking into administrative chaos. People scrounged for scraps of food. Russian officers were commandeering houses and taking over the choicest remaining buildings in Potsdam for their headquarters. There were widespread arrests, and daily reports of shootings and hangings. The number of Soviet staff cars evident in the streets increased by the hour, some with loudspeakers mounted atop them. The men and women of Potsdam had been ordered out to clear away the rubble in the streets. One morning, more than two hundred liberated American airmen, freed POWs marching in from the east, came shuffling right up Charlottenstrasse toward Sans Souci, where a string of American army trucks, arrived the night before from Halberstadt, were waiting to collect them. Nevertheless, for all the nervous activity, and the streets thronging with hard-drinking, loud Russian soldiers, the ending of the war had produced not only exhaustion but a palpable sense of relief. People like Ursula, toiling long hours, paused in the sun, making small talk. The planting of vegetable gardens was a common sight, as was the attempt by many Potsdamers to shore up and rehabilitate their houses. A railway engineer named Helmut Knitter, who gave Ursula some fresh milk in return for cigarettes, said that the cities of Germany were a devastation from one end to the other, from the Alps to the North Sea. The most beautiful of them all, Dresden, he said, no longer existed.

Ursula had heard about that. "I never saw Dresden," she said.

"Then you never will," he replied. "It does not exist anymore."

One afternoon, while Ursula was working in the streets with a cleanup squad of her neighbors, she allowed Ingeborg to take Andreas for a short walk. It was a bright, breezy day, with green shoots in evidence everywhere. There were signs of apple blossoms behind fences and walls, and lilacs showing here and there in parks and back yards; in places, one saw a blossoming bush or tree in the very midst of charred timbers. Ingeborg was going in the direction of Olivia Jupp's house. With her usual air of self-assurance and straight-mindedness, she had decided to go to Olivia's door and introduce herself. Somehow, having Andreas in tow made it seem less brazen and easier to do.

As she and Andreas turned into Lindenstrasse, which was crowded along its entire length with workers and soldiers shambling every which way, and a steady stream of vehicles threading slowly among the half-filled craters, a cheerful group of five or six Russian enlisted men stopped on the cobbled walkway to tease and play with Andreas. One of the soldiers tossed Andreas into the air. Ingeborg was frightened for a second or two by the suddenness of the action, but recognized at once the harmless good fun of it all. They were charmed by her baby brother.

For several minutes, the young men made good sport of the boy, tossing him up in the air and catching him. Andreas was squealing and laughing happily. With each whooping sound of the young men, as they caught him and flipped him higher, Andreas let out a whoop of his own. Ingeborg had never seen him so happy. People in the street stopped what they were doing to watch the impromptu spectacle. Two of the young soldiers began singing and clapping, giving voice to a lilting Russian folk ditty, while Andreas sailed above their heads. Ingeborg could not have framed it in thought, but in some part of her she wondered if perhaps Andreas didn't realize that a great anguish had passed, that the incessant dread of the night to come, with its pounding flak and the crashes, had — perhaps — ended here, being tossed in the air by friendly hands; that he might now become, at last, the innocent six-year-old boy that God had created him to be. He was giggling with joy and shrieking with every upward toss into the air. As he went up, he extended his arms like wings. Ingeborg looked on with a fixated smile. One of the Russian youths took Andreas by the wrists and swung him round and round in swooping arcs, while the others clapped and sang. Even after Ingeborg collected him, and they resumed their way, Andreas kept looking back, playing peekaboo with one of the withdrawing soldiers, a stout, red-faced young man who continued winking back at him through the crowds of passersby.

The effect of this moment of spontaneous gaiety upon Ingeborg was complex beyond her powers to understand it, but the look of happiness on Andreas's face moved her very deeply. At the next street corner, she stopped and put her hand over her eyes. She remembered that cold and dark night when he had wanted a potato; she remembered his joy on finding his chess set. She remembered the afternoon in Berlin when she saw him for the first time, brought home in a blanket as a newborn. A woman, on noticing Ingeborg crying, stopped and asked what was troubling her. Ingeborg shook her head, took Andreas by the hand, and crossed the street.

As luck would have it, she found Hansi Heiss with three or four of his teenage classmates standing about the steps of their bomb-damaged school. Ingeborg's heart jumped when she spotted Olivia among them. She made straight for them, leading Andreas.

"Look who is here," said Hansi, teasing her as she approached. "It's Ingeborg Maas, Frau Redeker's pet."

"I am not a teacher's pet," Ingeborg responded with the sort of primness which, she had learned, usually prompted more playful teasing of the sort she enjoyed. She turned at once, though, to Olivia, and could not conceal the look of childish admiration in her face. "I saw you tap dancing one day when I was with my mother."

"I remember you," said Olivia.

Ingeborg couldn't take her eyes from the girl. She loved the waviness of her dark hair, and her posture, which was board-straight, and the seriousness of her gray eyes. She was visibly infatuated with the Jupp girl, and wanted to be liked and admired in return. "It was a wonderful dance," she said.

Olivia was wearing a peasant-style dirndl, as were the girls, Fia Paust and Christiana Grewe, who were standing beside her. Ingeborg found herself wondering for a second if Olivia had burned her Hitler Youth uniform and concluded by instinct that she probably had not; that it was still hanging among her things; that was how she saw Olivia. Mostly, Ingeborg was searching her mind for something smart and ingratiating to say which would endear her to the fifteen-year-old, when, by good fortune, Hansi spoke up in an inadvertently helpful way.

"Ingeborg," he said, in that intentionally sissified voice contrived to tease her, his eyes going up, "reads big thick novels that weigh a ton and remembers every single word. She used to come up to our class every week."

Ingeborg looked round at all of them. Olivia, who had turned at the sound of a horn blowing, was smiling at Ingeborg from the tail of her eye. "You read novels?" she said.

"Romances are my favorites," Ingeborg was proud to respond. She couldn't stop looking at the older girl. "I could let you take some," she said.

"That's all right," said Olivia, unconcernedly.

If nothing else, Ingeborg was persistent. "Would you let me watch you dance again?"

"You remember where I live," Olivia remarked with a

smile. "You could come next Sunday afternoon at three o'clock."

"*I could?*" Ingeborg's sophistication abandoned her. "Oh, I will!" she exclaimed, thrilled at the ease with which she had carried off her coup. "Thank you. I'll come to your house at three o'clock."

Fia spoke up then, also teasingly, and in a suggestive voice, to Olivia. "Will Bübchen be there, also?"

Here, uncharacteristically, Olivia blushed. "I don't know," she answered.

Ingeborg spun round to Hansi. "Is Bübchen home?" she cried. "Your brother is home?"

"Yes," Hansi said, "he walked."

"Bübchen is a hopeless liar," said Christiana Grewe.

"He walked," said Hansi. "He walked from Cuxhaven."

"He *said* he walked," said Olivia.

"Well, he didn't fly."

"Bübchen is home?" To Ingeborg, Bübchen was the first soldier or sailor to come back from the front. The news was exciting, as it could prefigure now the return of others.

"He told me that he walked *backward*," said Christiana, with a contrived tolerance for congenital liars. "In case his sergeant spotted him, he said, he could pretend to be going the other way. He's a hopeless liar."

Ingeborg laughed gaily at the picture of the delightful Bübchen walking backward along the road for a hundred miles or more while pretending to be going the other way. She divined also that Olivia was either Bübchen's girlfriend, or, if not, that she would like to be. Ingeborg felt that they would be very nice together. They were her ideal of a romantic young couple. Everyone loved Bübchen, and Ingeborg hoped Olivia would win him.

Going home, with Andreas in hand, Ingeborg passed the

chapel where she used to stop in after school, and remembered the dismal day in January when she had stuffed the returned letter written to her father into the coin box. Farther along, she came upon her mother's work team. Ursula was wearing a pair of men's trousers and was sweated and very tired, but was happy to see the two of them. She had a small parcel of bread and butter, a week's rations, but had also acquired from a woman she had known at the Red Cross center a potato and a can of sardines. During this period, when the prospect of widespread starvation seemed real, there was no meat to be had. Even horsemeat was scarce to the vanishing point. At home, Ursula fried potato slices, while Ingeborg went down to the corner pump for water. It was about six o'clock, and getting toward twilight. Ingeborg's head was filled with thoughts about Olivia Jupp, and the return from the war of Bübchen Heiss — when something transpired before her eyes that made this day the most appalling of her life.

She had pumped the pail half full of water, and was just picking it up by the handle, when she saw the commotion develop outside Werner Welt's house. It started with a crashing sound, followed by the heart-stopping scream of a man. That was Werner. He was screaming. At the same time, she saw a Soviet Army truck parked across the street, a man at the wheel and the motor running. There was chicken wire stretched over the open back of the truck. One second later, the men came bursting through Herr Welt's front door, with Werner in their midst. Four Russian MPs were dragging and thrusting him along. One clutched Werner's arm behind his back. Another was pulling him like a sack by the shirt. Werner Welt's glasses were missing, and blood was flowing from his ear.

Ingeborg's body went cold. She was fixated in horror for one moment. Then she let go the pail handle and ran directly into the street. She wanted to put herself in Werner's way. She knew what was happening and wanted him to see her. Then his head struck the back of the truck with a sharp crack, and Ingeborg let out a scream. He was actually looking sideways at her, not six feet away now, as they threw him bodily over the tailgate. One of his shoes was off. There was a sudden long slice mark across the top of his forehead, from which blood poured over his eyebrows. Up close, Herr Welt's face was contorted with an anguish that was indescribable. She was right next to the truck. An MP shouted at her in Russian to get back! She didn't move until the truck itself began to roll. Her eyes were on Werner every second. He was staring back at her through the chicken wire with a look of unearthly astonishment. Blood was flowing over the bald top of his head, and he was clutching at the wire with his fingers. One of the MPs, climbing aboard, kicked the block warden in the stomach, as the truck jolted around the corner. He had turned again, twisting his head, and was looking back at her. Ingeborg followed as far as she could, running out into the middle of the street after him. She didn't know which way to go. She ran back toward his door in Jägerstrasse, then started back, running this way and that in the street. A pedestrian at the corner, a Russian soldier, tried to restrain and calm her. Ingeborg kicked viciously at his leg. She was beside herself with distraction. "They're wrong! They're wrong!" she cried. "That's Werner! He's bleeding. Somebody do something!"

She ran back past the pail of water she had left at the

pump, and fled to her door and up the stairs. Her mind was swimming. For many minutes, Ursula tried to quiet and soothe her. Within an hour, however, everyone along the street knew what had happened to the block warden. Within a quarter hour of his being dragged from his house, he was executed in public. Werner Welt and four other local Nazi officials were hanged to death from a tree in Wilhelm Platz.

When Ingeborg heard about it, she gave out a long, dolorous moan. She clapped her hand to the top of her head. He had not deserved that, she said. There were horrible people, who had done horrible things, but her neighbor, whom she loved, was not one of them. She sat in Ursula's lap, rocking to and fro. Werner's dark, perspiring face, and the blood upon him, and his missing glasses, haunted her mind all evening. In the morning, looking out the window at Herr Welt's naked garden, she saw where he had begun to assemble the gazebo. She looked down upon it with a drained expression. He must have done it yesterday. At the back of the garden space, stood three assembled sections of the octagonal gazebo, bolted together, standing forlornly by the wall, just where she had told him to put it up. Now, he would never come again into his garden. Her thoughts were full of him. She had noticed often how his house needed cleaning. She had noticed how his clothes needed ironing. He had needed a loving hand; now he was gone.

Ursula did not report to her work team that morning, but for Ingeborg's sake took both children to an early service at St. Peter and Paul's, in Bassin Platz. She tried constantly to assuage Ingeborg's grief, but without much luck. Ingeborg was thinking about the gazebo, and Werner's teacups, his gardening books, and the picture of Stephanie which he treasured. It was late morning before Ingeborg made any sensible outward statement whatever. They were standing in the sun outside the church.

"One day," Ingeborg said, making a soft oath of it to herself, "I will make *him* a garden."

Nevertheless, on Sunday, several days later, Ingeborg went at three o'clock to Olivia Jupp's house on Lindenstrasse. She came out the door like a young lady making a social call. Ursula and Andreas accompanied her most of the way, Ingeborg stepping along ahead of them. She wore her embroidered blouse, patent leather shoes, and had brushed her hair until it shone white-gold and silky. Her mother had given her a small purse to carry. There was something distinctly elfish and out of place in the sight of Ingeborg weaving her way through stacks of masonry rubble, past several bomb-demolished houses, the sun igniting her hair, her temples translucent. "I can go the rest of the way alone," said Ingeborg, as they approached Olivia's corner.

Understanding her daughter's vanity, her reluctance to arrive someplace with her mother as escort, Ursula acceded with a smile and turned back for home with Andreas. Ingeborg watched the two of them go before continuing. By the time she reached the door, she was thrilled from head to foot. Olivia's mother was instantly taken with her and whispered to the others present about the enchanting child. She liked the way Ingeborg sat forward on her hard chair by the piano, her hands folded over one another on her lap, her face a calculated opalescent blank. Olivia had two younger sisters, one of whom, named Gretl, was only a year younger than Ingeborg. Ingeborg made a point of being very prettily polite whenever Gretl spoke to her, but it was a politeness as glacial and unencouraging as she could make it. She could not allow herself to be classified as a peer of Olivia's little sister. On an occasion when Gretl showed Ingeborg an old prewar book of paper dolls and paper dresses, Ingeborg regarded it sidelong, without averting her head even an eighth of an inch. Gretl inquired whether Ingeborg liked paper cutouts. Ingeborg scarcely moved her lips. "No," she said, and returned her attention to the others in the room, once and for all.

In the course of things, Olivia presented a modest dance recital. Her grandparents Jupp, who lived in an apartment at the back of the house, had entered and were sitting side by side on a high-backed bench by the window. There were several children present. Fia, Olivia's friend at school, arrived last of all, and was greeted warmly by all present. Herr Jupp, Olivia's father, sat in a big brocade chair close to Ingeborg. He was a handsome, stockily built man, with wavy hair and furry eyebrows; he sat back with his legs crossed, chewing on the amber mouthpiece of the empty pipe he clutched in his fist and looking every inch the part of the senior civil servant. He had been the postal director in Potsdam for years. More than once, he nodded amiably to Ingeborg. She tried not to look at the big family picture standing on the credenza behind him, as she knew that the three boys in the picture were all dead. Olivia's mother was playing the piano softly all the while; she played creditably well. Despite the fact that big patches of plaster were missing here and there on the walls, the house was impressive to Ingeborg's eye, accustomed as she was to living in cramped quarters.

In the next half hour, Olivia tap-danced to a series of lively airs selected by her mother. She danced on the hard oak floor right in front of the piano. While tap dancing might not have been one of Ingeborg's favorite performance arts, she was thrilled to watch Olivia doing it. Olivia seemed quite artful, too, in the way she produced changing facial expressions appropriate to the spirit of each succeeding piece. Other times, Olivia sat down with the others in the room and listened as her mother played longer, more lyrical pieces. Ingeborg recognized one such selection as something she had heard one Monday evening while listening with her mother to a live radio performance by the Berlin Philharmonic. The selection sounded very dreamy; unaccountably, it reminded Ingeborg all at once of the verbal picture her mother had drawn of her lovesick father on the day she found him waiting for her in the street outside her office, looking, she said, "like something that had been hit by lightning." The piece was called an "etude." Ingeborg liked the way that Frau Jupp, while playing, closed her eyes and appeared to be floating away on the buoyant motion of the music. Ingeborg felt wonderfully special all the while. She was enjoying herself no end. For one thing, the chair on which she sat was positioned slightly forward of everyone else's. That way, all the others, she hoped, would take notice of the look of profound concentration on her face, as well as of the dignity of her posture. She hoped especially that Olivia noticed.

After the recital, Olivia's grandfather went out of the room, and came back after some minutes with a bottle of red wine. The sight of the wine animated those on hand. Frau Jupp asked her father-in-law where he had come by such a treasure, and the grandfather remarked jovially that he had got it in a barter. "In exchange," he said, "for a Baroque music box, a swan, and three horses."

Olivia's father in the meanwhile had initiated a conversation with Ingeborg.

"We are all very pleased to have a new guest," he said.

Ingeborg responded in her most pleasing manner. She was on a cloud. She liked the spacious house, she loved the attention, and she loved Olivia. "I am very pleased that Olivia invited me."

"You are very ladylike, Ingeborg," said Herr Jupp, at one point, as though he had been reading her mind.

In thanking him, Ingeborg showed him a smile that did nothing to dismiss or refute his compliment. She was further gladdened when she saw how Olivia's mother had diluted the wine in all the children's glasses with a half portion of water, while pouring Ingeborg's own little glass ruby red to the top. She hoped Gretl had noticed.

The picture of Ingeborg holding her wineglass in both hands above her knee, while maintaining a discussion of her future plans with Olivia's father, was a sight to behold.

"How did you decide upon the book business?" Herr Jupp desired to know. He was very taken with the sophisticated girl.

"It was my father's idea that I should become a bookseller," she replied. "He thought that would make me happy."

"I agree that it's a wonderful idea."

"Will it be possible, Herr Jupp," she asked, in adult accents, "for people to live in the capital again?"

He opened his hands. "They are living there today."

"I mean for a bookseller." For the first time, Ingeborg paused to sip from her wine. She couldn't wait to describe the afternoon to her mother.

"The city will be rebuilt," he said.

"Will it be as it was?" she asked. Then she added, "I was born in Berlin."

"Ah!" He nodded genially, as if expressing admiration at such a claim. "I didn't know that."

"We lived on Fasanenstrasse. My father said that Kurfürstendamm would be a wonderful street for bookselling."

"I am sure he is right about that, Ingeborg."

Ingeborg looked down evasively. "He would like to do it with me," she added. She could not recall for certain how much of her recollection was factual and how much imagined.

"A father-and-daughter business could be very enjoyable and make you a satisfying life. Maybe you," he said, "would order all the books and sell them, while your father could take care of the bills and paperwork."

"That was how I imagined it," she confessed. "I would like to pick out all the books."

"Your father," Herr Jupp added, with feeling, "is very lucky to have you."

Hearing that, Ingeborg started to respond, but abruptly ran out of words. Her sophistication deserted her. She could say no more about her father, and sat inertly, staring into space. Olivia's father noticed instantly the change that had come over the girl, and signaled to his daughter to come help. He divined at once, correctly, the origins of her changed behavior, and excused himself.

When Olivia sat down beside her, Ingeborg was gaping at the wineglass on her lap, while rocking slightly forward and back on her chair. She looked momentarily babyish, an impression heightened by the translucent pallor of her temples and cheeks. In fact, what had happened in the street five days ago, right before her eyes, to Werner Welt, had shaken her faith. Just talking about her father sent a cold shiver through her.

"Did you enjoy the music?" Olivia asked.

"Oh, I did." Ingeborg turned to Olivia with a thankful look. But unlike her usual self, she had nothing else to say. No thought or words came to mind.

Forewarned by her father that something was wrong, Olivia made conversation for both of them. She tap-danced, she explained to Ingeborg, mostly because her mother liked it.

Ingeborg's mind remained a blank, but she was capable of reacting to simple utterances. "You dance beautifully," she said, and stared at the older girl. She liked looking into Olivia's eyes; they were an oceanic gray, with a pale, steady light burning inside them, and they contained something intimate, a desire to understand. Ingeborg liked Olivia even better than Betka. Betka was, it proved, frivolous. Ingeborg felt her strength coming back, and with it a resurgence of faith in a fulfilling future. Ingeborg did something then over which she might later have marveled. She set aside her glass, and took Olivia's hand in both of hers, and squeezed it while speaking. "I'm so happy you invited me to your house today. I admire you very much." Sometimes candor came easily. "I'm happy, too, that you didn't run away. Everybody else did."

"I know," said Olivia.

Ingeborg was no longer at a loss for words, and allowed her heart to speak. She was clasping and squeezing Olivia's hand. "I think you're very strong and beautiful. I would be honored to be your friend. I can't dance," she said, "and I can't play music, and I can't act on a stage or make people laugh. I like to go to school. I like to read books. I'd like to be able to call you Olivia."

"I am Olivia."

"May I call you that?" Ingeborg was openly enamored of the older girl, but was herself in no way unimpressive to the other. Olivia was touched by what she was hearing.

"You're beautiful, Ingeborg."

"Thank you."

"Please call me Olivia."

"I saw you in the queue at the food shop one day when you shouted at somebody."

"I remember."

"I'm sorry about your brothers, Olivia." Ingeborg had an impulse to kiss Olivia's hand, but resisted it.

Ingeborg's heart was flooded with crosscurrents too tumultuous and profound to be contained in its shores. She struggled daily, even hourly, to be strong in her faith. She sought strength where she could find it. Sometimes it seemed that every moment was a fight. Here, she succumbed to her prevailing feelings, the passions of the moment, as she lifted Olivia's hand and kissed her fingers.

Ingeborg was more than delighted to have been admitted into Olivia's world. Before the Russian troops had come pouring into Potsdam, she had worried that the arrival of the enemy would have opened a still darker era in her life. But now, even while there was talk of widespread starvation, she felt nonetheless the meaning of the word "peace" inside herself. The endless droning formations of bombers, night and day, throughout memory, had slipped away at last into an enduring silence. The smell of gas in the streets was gone, as was that sickly sweet stench of bodies buried among the ruins. It was during this hour that Ingeborg made up her mind to begin going daily to the railway station. She determined also not to be dissuaded or prevented from doing so.

Many soldiers were straggling home by now. They came on foot, by rail, even by horse and cart. While the trains across the country were not operating on any schedule but were simply ordered from place to place by trainmasters on the spot, late afternoon in Potsdam nearly always found a freight train or two arriving in the station. In some cases, wounded were removed from one train or another. The station was usually crowded. There was a constant milling about of Russian soldiers, of civilians hoping to catch a ride someplace, or awaiting the arrival of a loved one.

Ingeborg thanked Olivia Jupp profusely for the invitation to her recital, made a point of bidding a pleasant goodbye to Olivia's parents and her grandparents, and departed for home. Hansi, who was just arriving, walked Ingeborg as far as the Kanal, from which point she continued alone. She did not go directly home, however, but started off toward the train station. It was warm walking in the late afternoon sun by the little Kanal, with the waters flowing dark underneath the bridge, an undulant movement, reflecting in flashes the blue of the sky, and the trees in leaf now from the botanic garden across the way. Ingeborg looked at herself in the water. She held onto the iron-pipe fence and watched her face form and dissolve on the dark mirror of the water. She recalled the afternoon in the Stettin Station in Berlin, two summers ago, the thousands of men on the platform, the air filled with cigarette smoke, the roar of all their voices, and how he, her father, appeared older than his companions. She remembered his face when he came toward her. It was a big and forbidding place. It was not a good place from which to have said goodbye.

Ingeborg took a longer route to the station. She did not want to see Wilhelm Platz, where Werner had been hanged. As long as she lived, she promised herself, she would never set eyes on that horrible, grisly tree. This week, whenever Werner's sweated, bloodied face had come pressing forward in her mind, staring in torment at her through the chicken wire, she suppressed it. As she passed the ruins of the Garrison Church, she saw a Russian woman openly nursing her baby. By the Langen Bridge, a woman was trying to exchange a beautiful silver-beaded dress and matching silver shoes to anyone lucky enough to be carrying something to eat. Ingeborg crossed the bridge to the station, stepping along expeditiously.

On the platform, a family of four were washing themselves at a water pump. Up the tracks could be seen workmen repairing a section of damaged rails. Cars were being uncoupled noisily, and an engineer was shouting instructions to a railroad worker who was walking toward him along the top of the train. The man walking on the cars was carrying a long black crowbar in one hand, with three enormous metal lanterns dangling from the other. No one was disembarking from either of the trains. The afternoon shadows grew long in the station. There was a feeling of evening coming on in the quality of the sounds, growing ever more resonant under the dome of a dimming sky. It gave Ingeborg a chill. Before long, she started for home.

As she walked into the Lustgarten, past the regimental barracks, she was thinking about the difference between what was true, and what others thought was true. She was thinking about what they did not know; because she knew that if her father had actually died, he would have died inside of her. She would have felt it happen one day. She would have been talking with Frau Redeker at school, or standing in a queue by a food shop, and it would have happened. It would have occurred inside her. Something big, heavy, and cold would have moved down slowly inside of her, quite unexpectedly, right beside her heart, when he died, and would have stayed there for days and days.

She was walking close to the buildings, her head down, absorbed in her thoughts. At the corner of her own street, an exotic two-wheeled Russian droshky came clattering past on the cobbles, its cherry red spokes blurring, the horse neighing and shaking its head vivaciously. Ingeborg didn't even notice. With her eyes on the ground, she turned in at her doorway.

That afternoon, while Ingeborg was visiting Olivia, her mother had met Herr Haberzettl in the street. Tonight, he came to call. He was such a cheerful soul, and his visit was very welcome. He brought a bottle of schnapps and some little cakes. One day soon, said Felix, if Providence was kind, he might be allowed to open some form of restaurant. With a glass of schnapps before him, he portrayed a sense of calm and well-being. His personality influenced the entire room. Ingeborg liked him very much, especially as she recalled what grand fun it had been going out to dinner that winter night, and how the youthful Franzi had flirted with her, and even excited feelings of romantic love in her. She also knew that Herr Haberzettl was attracted to Ursula. She could tell by the way the restaurateur looked at her mother, with a fixed half smile on his face and a soft light in his eyes. Nor was Ingeborg unaware that her mother had made herself more attractive that evening, by wearing her best spring dress, and serving the cakes just so, with the small plates and little silver forks that she rarely had cause to use anymore.

Herr Haberzettl held Andreas on his lap from time to time, teasing and fondling the boy in a fatherly way. Ingeborg could be remarkably insightful at such moments; she easily saw through the goings-on, but she didn't care. She liked seeing her mother happy. She liked also seeing her moving about in her best dress, with her hair brushed, and her beautiful smile igniting again and again. No one had so beautiful a smile. More than once, Ingeborg found herself gazing lengthily at her mother. She suspected that it was Fräulein Ursula Schechter's smile that had caused Walter Maas to fall in love with her, want to marry her, want to mingle his dust with hers.

Often spontaneous, Ingeborg spoke it out. Her words came as softly as a lover's.

"You're very beautiful, Mommy."

"Oh, my!" Ursula had just seated herself at the table, pulling up her chair. She looked round at all of them. "I am so complimented."

Ingeborg persisted relentlessly, staring at her, still entranced. "You are," she said.

Ursula blushed noticeably, especially as her daughter's passionate observation was so frank. She turned to Herr Haberzettl. "In the hardest times," she said, "God creates the most precious children. I think that all over the world the dearest children that God ever made are being made now, in our time." She looked down at her plate. "I have two of them."

Being a man of expansive good cheer by profession, the restaurant man intentionally steered the conversation toward more frivolous topics. He wanted to see Andreas's chess set. He showed the little boy how to arrange the pieces on his makeshift chessboard. He explained to Ingeborg that chess was an ancient Persian game. It was a logical contest, he told her, with no element of luck in it.

"I would not like a game without luck," she replied, in that conclusive, pert way of hers which left little room for rebuttal. "If there isn't luck in it," she added, "it isn't even a game. How could it be? Soccer," she pointed out, "is a game where a player can trip in the mud. Pinochle is a game because you don't know what cards you will get. Hide-and-seek," she went on, instructively, "is a game because there are so many places to hide, and there are *different* places to hide when you play the game in different places."

"Ingeborg is lecturing," said Ursula.

"And," Ingeborg added, "I am right."

"I wouldn't disagree for the world," said Felix, beaming over the girl's pedagogical performance.

Ingeborg got up from the table to light the lamp. "That," she said of the chess set, "is arithmetic."

"It is not," Andreas spoke up suddenly in an irritated tone. "It's a game!"

Ingeborg showed her brother a simpering, mechanical smile. "It's very pretty," she said, switching on the lamp, and returning to her seat.

"It's a game," said Andreas, his eyes following her in resentment.

"If you like it, it's a game," said Ursula. "If you don't like it, it's not a game."

"I don't like it, or *not* like it," Ingeborg exploited the fissure in her mother's reasoning, showing Ursula her expressive eyes.

Herr Haberzettl laughed aloud. "You are right, Frau Maas. God has been working harder than ever."

Before going, Felix remarked on the recent increase in the number of military policemen in the streets of Potsdam.

"I have noticed them," Ursula replied.

"There's going to be a historic conference here," he said. "Stalin, Churchill, all of them. Which is a good thing for Potsdam. The Russians will probably want us civilians to look decent and healthy."

Ursula saw him downstairs to the door. They exchanged pleasantries. In parting, Herr Haberzettl kissed Ursula's hand. She watched as he made his way up Charlottenstrasse. Ursula remained a while at her doorstep. Darkness had fallen, but the sky was moonlit. Above the bomb ruins, she could make out the shattered dome of St. Nicholas's a half mile away. She remembered their first Sunday here, and the dejection on Ingeborg's face when she explained to her that they would be living from now on in the room above Annaliese Falke's apartment. She took the children out that afternoon to look at Potsdam for the first time. It was a summer day in 1943. They sat on the stone steps by the Havel, not far from the colonnade of the town palace. There were three swans on the water that day. The water was bright and black, and the beautiful birds, snowy, sculpted, austere, ominous, floated upon it, living presentiments of a dark age to come. The familiar past, with everything in it that Ursula had put together and cherished, had been taken away forever.

From afar, came the deep organ note of an airplane. Ursula watched as the aircraft traversed the stars, its wing lights blinking.

Upstairs, after the children were asleep, Ursula searched out an envelope of snapshots from among her things and went through them slowly, one by one. Her eyes lingered over the baby pictures of Ingeborg. In one photo, her favorite, taken when her daughter was three, Walter was holding her up in the crook of his arm; Ingeborg was tracing her finger down the line of her father's nose; with her other hand behind him she held a white balloon on a string; the balloon floated moonlike above their two heads.

There was only one snapshot of the four of them taken together. In it, Ursula looked very bourgeois, with her floppy felt hat, her long woolen coat, and square-heeled shoes. Walter was beaming at the camera. At their feet, Andreas was tugging at Ingeborg's sleeve. Ursula stared at Andreas in the picture. He was such a sweet boy, a thankful boy, always willing and compliant. These were the children of the storm. These were the little ones of whom heroism was required as a simple matter of course. Not just to learn to dress themselves, or how to brush their hair, but to be heroic, night and day, winter and spring, in the full epical meaning of the word; in the old high meaning of the word. She remembered the sight of Andreas in the red glare of the rectory cellar on the night of the great devastation, his hair standing straight up on end. She had got a description, too, of Ingeborg chasing the truck with the chicken wire on it, saying, "He's bleeding!" Ursula's eyes lingered on the sight of her two heroes asleep in their beds, and guessed there was surely a grand new age to come. How could that not be true?

Ursula collected the pictures in her hands, squared them off, and put them back into the envelope. That done, she put her head down on the table and indulged her feelings.

As things came about, that day had marked the beginning of Ingeborg's regular pilgrimages to the train station. She went every day, as though keeping an appointment. The

knowledge that Ingeborg was doing so, and that she would
not bow to motherly advice or prohibitions, deepened Ursula's suffering. She wished Ingeborg was like other children
in that way, and suspected, probably wisely, that it was the
peculiar combination of childish innocence and precocious
brilliance that made the girl not only headstrong but probably more vulnerable than others to severe disappointment.
There were times when Ursula actually worried that a day
would come soon when Ingeborg might be so broken by the
realization of what had in fact happened to her father, and to
her unbounded confidence in his return, that she might try
to destroy herself. That was not an idle worry. Ursula saw
her daughter as the sort of volatile child capable of doing
just that. Without Ingeborg beside her, the future was unthinkable.

In time, she pleaded with Ingeborg. She sought to devise
ways whereby she could gradually accustom the girl to the
possibility, even a remote one, of disappointment. She
scarcely dared try, however. She saw the certitude in the
jewel-like eyes, which, when sensing a challenge, turned sus-
picious and recriminatory. Twice, when the mother strove
to discourage Ingeborg's waiting on the platform at the
S-Bahn station, she noticed, as an irony, that her daughter's
confidence, unlike another's in such a circumstance, actually mounted. "He's alive," said the daughter. She said it
twice.

One afternoon that week, Ingeborg saw a mother reunited
with her son in the station. The ex-soldier was missing a leg
and had to be helped from the train. It was the S-Bahn from
Berlin, and was crowded with civilians and Russian soldiers.
People thronging streetward regarded the mother and son
sympathetically as they hurried by. The woman was beside

herself with joy, blurting her son's name over and over again, while clutching at his clothes in a kind of disbelief, as though he were something returned to her from the beyond. In nearly the same moment, though, an argument broke out between two Russian soldiers, and escalated in moments into a fistfight. Soviet MPs pushed their way through the crowd. The two soldiers, in their fighting, careened their way onto the tracks. When the military policemen interfered, both soldiers turned and began at once punching the MPs. The MPs were swinging their sticks. The violence sickened Ingeborg. It sent her hurrying from the station.

It was raining outdoors. Bicyclists coming from the bridge came past with their heads down. A full streetcar pulled away from the station, its wipers going, the roof gleaming. Others with umbrellas up waited for the next tram. Ingeborg could not see very far in the rain. The sky was low and leaden. She walked out across the glistening cobbles as far as the Langen Bridge, and then stopped and turned back. She couldn't make up her mind. It had been an article of faith with her for some while that her father could arrive at the station only at a time when she was there waiting for him. With that in mind, not wishing to waste a day, she walked back across the cobbles. As she did so, she saw the two soldiers who had been brawling being hauled out by the Russian MPs into the street. One of the two soldiers continued to struggle, and was being struck again and again about the head and shoulders with a stick. Ingeborg hesitated. She felt frightened and discouraged.

She was standing in the drizzle outside the station, heedless of the people coming out and pushing past her, and did not notice for many long seconds the person standing nearby. It was a young Russian army officer. He was regarding her with concern. He held a big khaki umbrella above his head. His German was perfectly clear.

"Is something wrong?" he asked her.

Ingeborg stood in the rain. Her hair and bare arms were wet. The officer stood next to one of the ornate lampposts. He had been watching her for minutes. Ingeborg noticed, oddly, that he had dark brown eyes, even though wisps of blond hair protruded from the sides of his leather-billed officer's cap. He was short in stature and stood exceedingly straight, holding the umbrella handle in front of his shoulder. He was waiting for a reply.

"No," said Ingeborg. The flashes on his shoulder identified him as a lieutenant. His eyes were indulgent.

"Are you lost?" he said.

Ingeborg shook her head. "I live on Charlottenstrasse."

"You're waiting for someone?"

Ingeborg liked his looks. She liked the correctness of his bearing, and the politeness of his manner. He stepped forward then, smiling, and held the umbrella over her.

"I was waiting for my father," she replied truthfully.

The lieutenant nodded, closing his eyes, and then posed another question. He was condescending in a playful way. "Why don't you go into the station, then?" If the Russian had a daughter of his own not so different from the girl before him, it would well have explained his obvious solicitude.

"I don't think I will wait any longer today," she said, unaware of the perplexing nature of her response.

A longish moment passed before he spoke again; but he was looking at her nostalgically. "You wait for Papa," he said, "every day?"

"Yes," she said.

"He works with the railway?"

"No."

"Where is he working?"

"He is not here," Ingeborg admitted. "He was in the army in the east."

The Russian was standing quite close to her. He fiddled with the catch on his umbrella, moved his chin about as though the collar of his tunic was too tight, and looked at her again. "And you come here every day?"

"Yes," she said.

A vehicle passing in the street sent up a spray of water. He drew Ingeborg aside. "Has he told you that he's coming?"

"No." Ingeborg's eyes went to the entrance to the station.

"Then why do you wait every day?"

Ingeborg knew her response to be unreasonable, but said it anyway. "Because I know he is coming," she said.

The lieutenant returned the salute of several enlisted men walking past. "I am Lieutenant Severinsky," he said to her. "What's your name?"

Ingeborg liked his formality. "I am Ingeborg Maas."

"Well, I am very pleased to meet you." He nodded again playfully. "I think you are too wet, Ingeborg, to stay outdoors any longer. I will take you home," he said, "and then I'll come back and wait for your father."

Ingeborg agreed, as she was ready now to go home, anyway. She started along on his left, which required Lieutenant Severinsky to reach across his chest with the umbrella. Surprisingly, as they stepped into the street and started for the bridge, Ingeborg slipped her hand into his. Before they had gotten very far, however, Ingeborg balked. "I can't go this way," she said. She faltered. "There is a tree in the Wilhelm Platz —"

"A tree?" He looked at her.

"Some people were hanged there."

"*Ah!*" He understood perfectly. "Then we," he said, "shall find another street to go on. You lead us a better way."

The Russian had a very confiding nature, she could tell. She led them through Schwertfegerstrasse to the Kanal. She stole looks at him now and again. He was very interested in his surroundings. "This is a very pleasant route to have come by," he said. "I like the Kanal best of all."

"So do I," said Ingeborg.

"It's small," he said. "It's not like a watercourse, at all."

"It's pretty," said Ingeborg.

"It's like a decoration," he said.

She had taken his arm now. She thought she had never seen anyone with brown eyes and blond hair before. She liked the way he held the umbrella across his chest for her. It was very snug underneath. The rain pattered on it. Ingeborg wanted the Russian officer to appreciate her social skills, her ability to be both diverting and informative. "Before the bad bombing, there were rowboats tied up here. That's why there are stairs cut in the stone," she explained. She showed him a blue flash of her intelligent eyes.

They had stopped on the bridge. Lieutenant Severinsky smiled faintly as he peered down into the twinkling, slow-moving waters.

"What kind of trees are those?" He signified the trees that leaned over the Kanal.

Ingeborg had no idea whatsoever what species they were. "Lindens," she said.

He nodded interestedly.

As always, Ingeborg enjoyed putting her brilliance on display. "Where is your home?" she asked politely.

"In Russia," he said.

"Yes," said Ingeborg, a little tartly, and showing him her eyes, "but *where?*"

"I come from Tula. It's a city near Moscow. I was educated as an automotive engineer."

"You make automobiles?" She looked up at him, as they came away from the little bridge, strolling past the boys' and girls' high school where the rescue workers had stored the dead bodies the night of the great air raid.

"Mostly," Lieutenant Severinsky explained, "engineers make designs. They make exact plans on paper for every single part that is going to be made."

"Like blueprints?"

"That's exactly right, Ingeborg. You're very intelligent, aren't you?"

She was still walking on his arm. She contemplated her reply. "Yes," she said, "probably. Are there automobile plants in Tula?"

"Many were moved away because of the war," he said.

That remark puzzled Ingeborg. "How can an entire plant be moved?" she asked.

"Well," he stated, and nodded, "the machines are taken out of a building, put then on a train, taken far away to someplace safe, and there put into another building."

She made a pleasant noise in her throat. She liked learning things. "When you leave the army, will you go to Tula or to the new place where the auto plants are? *Or,*" she specified, smartly, "will they bring the plants back to Tula?"

"I will just go to some car factory that needs an automotive engineer. Wherever that may be."

Pausing momentarily as a sudden breeze sent down a

shower from the leaves overhead and set the waters of the
Kanal rippling, Ingeborg took the opportunity to look up at
him again and examine him. She found his chestnut brown
eyes and blond eyelashes a trifle shocking to her senses. "Do
you have a wife?" she asked.

"I was supposed to be married," he replied, with a kind of
Slavic fatalism, "but the woman married somebody else."

Ingeborg grew flirtatious. "She was probably not very intelligent," she said, and showed Lieutenant Severinsky the
corner of her eyes. The Russian laughed. She liked the way
he could be both airy and reserved at the same time. She
liked even more than that the protective way he favored her
with the umbrella. Ingeborg came up to his shoulder in
height, so she didn't have to look *up* at him, as from the dis-
advantage of a small child, while making conversation. As
they turned now into Hoditzstrasse, Ingeborg was walking
very straight and primly. She was sure they made a nice figure together. At this point, she did, however, giggle, asking
him, "Is her husband quite stupid?"

"Not at all." The Russian's self-deprecating irony seemed
somehow to deepen his voice. "We were all students together five years ago!" He gestured philosophically. "What
was I to do?"

"You were a university student five years ago?"

"Sometimes," said the lieutenant, thoughtfully, "I think
that I would like to teach automotive engineering."

Ingeborg lit up instantly. She stopped walking. "That
would be wonderful! You would be a professor! That's a
magnificent plan!"

"Do you think so?"

"Oh, yes." She was pulling at his arm. "That's what you
should do. That's better than making cars."

"And I like languages," he said, unaware that the enthusiasm of the pretty ten-year-old at his side was bringing him out. "I speak some German, and some English, and some French."

"You could teach all of those things!" she said. "You would be so respected! You could teach engineering, you could teach languages, and you could travel a lot, and write books about it, and about lots of things. I think you have wonderful ideas," she said. She showed him again that secretive look. "That woman would be so jealous," she said.

"She would be if I did all those things!"

At Ingeborg's door, Lieutenant Severinsky noticed the severe damage sustained on one side of the building. "Your house is safe?" he said.

"Yes," said Ingeborg. "Part of it was jacked up." But she was not thinking about that. For the first time in her life, Ingeborg was straining in her thoughts to conceive the proper way to say goodbye to a man who had escorted her home. She could offer her hand to be shook in parting. Or she could stand just so, very straight-spined, and express both her gratitude for his show of kindness and her pleasure at making his acquaintance today. Before she could decide which was the more ladylike and appealing, however, she noticed the change that came over him.

"I would like to speak to your mother," he said.

Although taken by surprise, Ingeborg did as instructed, and went upstairs to get Ursula. Lieutenant Severinsky waited inside the downstairs door. He closed his umbrella and took off his cap. Their voices sounded overhead. A full minute elapsed. Then the door opened by the head of the stairs, and Ursula appeared and came down the steps. Her eyes were wide with apprehension.

He reached to shake her hand. "It is nothing official," he

assured her. "I'm Lieutenant Severinsky. I found your daughter standing in the rain by the train station and brought her home."

"That was kind of you," Ursula responded to his words with relief. She remarked the formality of the young man. He had tucked his billed cap under his left arm and was holding the wet umbrella in hand, while remaining in place at the door.

"She's a very astute girl," he said. "We had a pleasant talk."

"Thank you. Yes," Ursula agreed, "she's advanced intellectually. She was always ahead of the others, even as a baby."

He seemed to Ursula to understand. "You are worried about her," he said, half asking and half asserting it.

"Very much," Ursula confessed. "She goes there every day." She looked up the stairs. The door was open an inch. The lieutenant had noticed also; with a glance, he signified the open door to Fräulein Falke's downstairs parlor. "Could we speak in there?"

"Yes." Ursula led the way. The few furnishings that remained in the room were scattered and overturned about the floor.

"No one lives here?" he asked in surprise, and looked about.

"They owned the house. They were a brother and sister," Ursula explained. "He was killed at the front, and she, the lady, was killed in the cellar. I scarcely knew them."

"Why don't you move down here?" he exclaimed, in a biggish voice. "This is a wonderful house!"

"I couldn't do that." Ursula reacted with wonder. "It isn't my house."

"It isn't anybody's house! It . . . it belongs to the Soviet

Union. Move your things down." He waved a hand of dismissal at the world outside the windows. "Who will know?"

The thought of doing such a thing had never occurred to Ursula. She didn't think in such ways.

"In Russia," he added, "the people would have moved in from upstairs while the corpses were still warm."

Ursula laughed embarrassedly over that.

Lieutenant Severinsky stepped to the front window, looked out at the street, and looked once more about the room. Ursula admired his correctness and the way he bore himself physically. The Russian soldiery she saw in the street was coarse and messy by comparison.

For several minutes then, speaking in undertones, Ursula explained her daughter's behavior.

The Russian was nodding, a trifle cynically. "She will become accustomed to what has happened," he said.

"I'm afraid she will not," said Ursula. "She is becoming less accustomed to it. I remember something dreadful that happened when I was a child. That was in Hambach," she explained, "near Aachen. There was a fourteen-year-old girl named Blanche Lorenz. I still remember her name. She was so brilliant she was allowed to take some university tests. She studied every hour of every day and was positive how well she was going to do when the time came. She had even saved up her money to buy a special leather schoolbag for her university days. One day her father, a lumber dealer, found her in his shed, hanging. She had failed her tests. She had climbed onto a stack of lumber and fixed the rope around her neck."

The young Russian, who had seen more suffering and death in the past four years than probably all his ancestors put together since the Middle Ages, took a colder view of things.

"Frau Maas," he said, "your daughter is not going to fail any tests. I think you both need more to eat."

"I shouldn't worry?" she asked hopefully, close to tears. "Because I do. Ingeborg is my life. I couldn't go on. I would not be able to go on without her. I have an overwhelming fear that that is how my world is going to end. Everything points to it. What a hard and brutal time it is to be a mother." In a characteristic gesture, Ursula held her hand to her forehead.

"Collect yourself," he snapped, impatiently.

"Out of love," she said, "we bring them to pass, and then love them more than God loves His own world. It is true," she said. "Mothers have more love in them than God. That's the tragedy. That's the heart of the nightmare. How could it not be true, if we love them more than life itself?"

Ursula was visibly distracted. She stood in the middle of the empty parlor, her fingers to her temples. "We lived in three pretty rooms on Fasanenstrasse in Berlin. My husband was a printer. He played soccer on Saturday afternoons. We had friends. I had two babies. The sun shone every day. What happened?"

Lieutenant Severinsky stepped toward the hall door. "You invaded Russia," he said. "That's what happened."

"Did I?" she inquired softly.

He took his umbrella in hand. "Well, somebody did," he said.

"Because if I did, I don't remember having done so."

Looking up, the Russian officer saw Ingeborg standing on the stairhead. At that distance, in the failing light, Ingeborg gave off a spectral, waifish look, her feet side by side, her heron-like legs touching. She had been standing there all the while. Her mother appeared to view from the parlor door. The sight of the two of them below did not incite a response from her. She had heard every word they said.

The Russian officer, on spotting her, could not forgo a humorous remark on departing. He spoke up the stairs to Ingeborg. "I'm glad you didn't invade Russia," he said. He turned to Ursula. "I am going to send someone over here with some rations."

"Thank you."

Ingeborg continued to survey them with a dispassionate expression. She offered Lieutenant Severinsky no sign or word of farewell as he put on his service cap. In fact, she saw the young man in uniform as similar to her mother in certain critical ways. That is, she saw neither of them as equal to the solitary and perilous dictates that drove her own heart. She knew herself to be her father's salvation; there was no other word for it.

The next day, she was out on the platform at the train station, the same as always, waiting.

In truth, the idea of killing herself had in fact entered Ingeborg's mind more than once. It was a thought that held no special fear for her, as the prospect of a world without her father, or a world that had concealed him from her, was not so different from no world at all. She had thought about that. She had thought about it sometimes during the bombings, when concussive blasts seemed to compress her down to the size of an insect, the sight of her brother quaking in the aftermath, his tongue lolling. She had thought about sleeping endlessly, lying in bed on one side of her mother, with

Andreas on the other, and the three of them just drifting
away into a limitless, peaceful sleep, and how much better
that would be than never to have him back, than never to
return to Berlin, never to be the bookseller with him, or ever
to be again his love and his joy.

But that was not how it was. He was, she knew, in the
world. He was not hidden behind wire, like the heartbreak-
ing, famished souls she saw in the pictures of the camps in
the Berlin *Zeitung* newspaper; he was not being marched
away in some snowy waste beyond tall, thousand-mile-off
mountains in the east; he lay not dead and overlooked in
some unspecified field. That was not how it was. There was
a train coming. The sky there was very big; there was a
farmhouse; there was water and tall grasses. The train rolled
on smoothly. She even knew where it was coming from. It
was coming from the north.

Sometimes, she recognized faces at the station; faces of
those who, she guessed, were doing what she was doing.
That made sense. They were doing what they were supposed to do. She was doing what she was supposed to do.
She was waiting for him. From here, he had gone away; to
here, he would one day return. And with every passing day,
she was more certain. She knew how he would look. He
would look tired, dusty, unwell.

Freight trains were her favorite because the men coming
back hitched rides with the engineers. She had learned that.
She had learned quite a lot about trains these past weeks.
The S-Bahn passenger trains, while loaded with people,
were not promising. The best ones were the trains with supplies on them, the noisy, smoky trains, out of which, every
day, a few straggling men emerged. Sometimes, they got off
just to stretch their limbs, get some water, maybe look

about, then climb aboard again. They were all ex-soldiers. Their uniforms were in disarray. Most looked rather happy, casual, carefree. Some bore the marks of having been hit. They milled about idly. She would see them going forward to talk a moment with the engine driver, or sitting in the open door of a freight car, their legs hanging down. Some smoked cigarettes. One, she remembered, had a big pipe in his fist and blew up a great cloud of smoke with it. If there were not many people on hand, sooner or later they would notice the blond girl with the bird legs going up and down the platform looking in the cars, and call to her.

"Are you the civil district governor of Potsdam?" asked one, one day, calling to her in an attractive baritone.

But Ingeborg, always proper, did not encourage flirting. Still, her many trips to the station had given her a sense of fellowship with them. They knew, she suspected, why she was there; just as she knew where they had been, and where they were going. These were the souls that she looked for and understood. These were the homecoming lost souls of the war. It was they who brought her footsteps to the platform every day, as she knew her father to be one of them.

On this particular day, as Ingeborg was walking the length of a fifteen-car freight train, looking into each car, an S-Bahn pulled in from Berlin. Just before the passengers disembarked, she turned and looked all the way back to the locomotive of the freight train. There was smoke in the station; it came from a pile of burning tires not far away. She hadn't even noticed the smoke. She had grown up in a world of smoke and gas fumes. She was a creature of smoke and paid it no notice; but it was through the smoke that she saw him. A man stepped down from the locomotive — he was an ex-soldier — and then, behind that man, he, Ingeborg's father, stepped down. She saw the first man, who was shorter, lay the flat of his hand in an encouraging way on the back of the second man; then he handed the second man some papers.

Ingeborg was moving toward them in a dream state. The doors of the S-Bahn train opened then on her left, and the passengers came pouring out onto that side of the platform. Ingeborg kept to her right, hurrying in the direction of the locomotive. Not a hundred feet away, the first soldier was pointing and explaining something to the second, all the while resting his palm on the other's back. The second soldier nodded once or twice. Ingeborg's eyes were fixed upon him, like something she had conjured out of the atmosphere. The younger man climbed then back into the engineer's cabin of the locomotive; and the second turned on his heel in the direction toward which the first had pointed. He did not see Ingeborg hurrying toward him from three cars back. He looked disoriented; but before he could step away from the train, she was upon him. She blocked his way. She stood breathless before him. For a second, she couldn't speak.

Her senses were in disarray. Clasping his sleeve with the tips of her fingers, she couldn't frame a thought. Her heart was overflowing.

"It's me," she said.

To Walter Maas, the girl before him was the revenant in dreams. Hers was the face that came and went on the black, mirroring waters of the Baltic, seen a hundred times from a distant window; it appeared once in smoke above a frightening, vicious killing ground, when he could not move his limbs; he had seen her there, and he had seen her in the smile of a farm girl who helped him with his pipe. This was his daughter in the flesh.

The sleeve of his tunic was torn at the cuff; he had a rudi-
mentary beard; he looked weary. He looked just the way she
knew he would. He was the living picture of the closing of
the bitterest age there ever was.

From behind them came the grinding and echoing clanks
of cars being coupled or uncoupled. The S-Bahn passengers
crowded their way out to the street. The wind in the station
shifted, blowing the smoke upward. The freight train behind them began to move.

Raising her arms, Ingeborg put everything she had to say
to him in a breath. Her lips shook.

"I waited," she said.

When he leaned to receive her kiss, he spoke her name.
He said Ingeborg.

A lone soldier, standing in the doorway of an empty
freight car, watched them from behind, as he went slowly
by.

KÖNIGS - PARK WEG

CHAUSSEE NACH BORNIM

JÄGER

SUMMER PALACE

KAISER - WILHELM

Tower

SANSSOUCI

JUNKERSTR.

HAUPT WEG

BRANDENBURG

Tower

PARK

CHARLOTTE

HOHENZOLLERNSTR.

LINDENSTR.

Tower

BREITESTR.

M

LUISENSTR.

WAISENSTR.

ZEPPELINSTR.

Glindowsee

HERMANNS-
WERDER

Havel